BLACK LIGHT: SUSPENDED

MAGGIE RYAN

BLACK COLLAR PRESS

Published by Black Collar Press

Black Light: Suspended
Maggie Ryan

EBook 978-0-9982191-4-1
Print 978-0-9982191-8-9

Cover Art by Eris Adderly, http://erisadderly.com/

This book is a work of fiction. Names, characters, places, and incidents either are products of the author's imagination or are used fictitiously. Any resemblance to actual persons, living or dead, events, or locales is entirely coincidental.

This story takes place in the Black Light world created by Livia Grant and Jennifer Bene. Maggie Ryan graciously accepted the invitation to play in our naughty world and we thank her from the bottom of our hearts for lending us her talent by joining the Black Collar family.

First Electronic Publish Date, March 2017

ISBN: 978-0-9982191-4-1

❀ Created with Vellum

BLACK LIGHT SERIES

Infamous Love, **A Black Light Prequel** by Livia Grant

Black Light: Rocked by Livia Grant

Black Light: Exposed by Jennifer Bene

Black Light: Valentine Roulette by Eight USA Today and Bestselling Authors

Black Light: Suspended by Maggie Ryan

Black Light: Cuffed by Measha Stone

Black Light: Rescued by Livia Grant (coming summer 2017)

CHAPTER 1

"**Y**ou a cop?" he asked, holding the tip of the knife against her throat.

"Do I look like a cop?" Charlize answered with a smile, lifting her hand to lay her palm against his chest, acting as if the knife didn't exist.

"No, you look like one fine piece of ass, but that doesn't mean shit. I've watched a lot of cop shows. You could be wearing a wire."

"Really? And where exactly would I hide it?"

"Let's see, shall we?"

Charlize forced herself not to move or even blink. She stood perfectly immobile as he nicked the fabric of her dress, drawing the knife down, the razor sharp blade making short work of the garment. She remained still as he cut the narrow straps, sending the plum colored sheath to the floor.

"Satisfied?" she asked. His response was to sneer and give three quick strokes of the knife to destroy her bra, her breasts falling free.

"For such a skinny woman, you've got great tits," he said,

palming one and giving it a squeeze. "Nice and fat." When she didn't say anything, his feral grin disappeared.

"You should thank your master when he gives you a compliment." His fingers closed around her nipple and gave it a brutal twist.

Every cell in her body demanded she end this before it went any further. But, she had a job to do. Shrugging, she said, "I wasn't sure if you like your submissives silent or vocal."

Her response seemed to placate him, as he released her nipple after giving it another squeeze. The knife traveled slowly through the valley of her breasts and over her abdomen, the feel of the steel against her flesh raising goose bumps. He slid the blade beneath the waistband of her black lace panties and she held her breath.

"Don't move," he ordered.

Charlize had no intention of disobeying with the blade now pressed against her sex. She didn't release her breath until he grinned.

"Impressive." He didn't seem to expect a response as he slowly pulled the knife free. "You didn't even flinch." Another few swipes of the knife and her last barrier fell away. "Unless you've got a wire shoved up your cunt or ass, I guess you came to play." Charlize just gave him a smile. "I'm gonna have a lot of fun discovering what it takes to have you lose your cool."

He shoved his hand between her legs, fingers probing, nails scratching as he roughly fondled her. She'd bitten her tongue when he pushed two fingers into her but managed not to make a sound. Charlize felt a moment of fear she'd blown her mission before it had really begun at the look of puzzlement on his face.

Pulling his hand free, he looked at it and then at her. "Not even a drop."

Running her fingernail in a tight circle where his chest hair tufted above his unbuttoned shirt, she purred, "I'm sure a man such as yourself can take care of that little problem. Or do I need to find someone—"

"Hell, I love a challenge! Time to play." He grabbed her by the hair, pulling her after him as he strode towards a piece of equipment across the room that Charlize thought most likely hadn't been sanitized since it had been set in place.

When he told her to lay down as he reached for the cuffs attached to the apparatus, she said, "You won't need those." Sitting down, she allowed her eyes to widen and her lips to curl into a smile as she looked up at him. "Unless, of course, you doubt your ability to keep me interested."

He didn't respond, but did drop the cuffs, giving her a smirk. "Baby, I've never failed to have every bitch I've played with begging for more. Lie down on your belly."

While he walked to a beautiful antique cabinet standing against one wall, Charlize again scanned the room. If she ignored the fact that several of the 'guests' were engaged in sexual acts instead of conversation; that half the caterers were carrying trays holding bowls filled with pills of every color instead of canapés; that women wearing ridiculously high heels were holding mirrors where perfectly formed lines of white powder could be snorted through rolled up C-notes that were then tucked between breasts that pushed out of the tight red corsets they wore, well, she could imagine that she was at some high society party. She filed away details and descriptions, tucking the information into various folders in her head, forcing herself not to jump up when she saw Sorenson returning, a thick wooden paddle in his hand.

"Time for you to meet the *ass buster*." He leered down at her as he ran his free hand over her bare ass. "Let's see how tough you are, shall we?" The first stroke told her that she was in for a grueling test of wills.

Charlize didn't know how much more she could stand before she blew. Digging her fingernails into her palms had stopped helping. It wasn't the strokes against her ass the man was continuing to give her that had her on edge, it was the constant spewing of inane words.

Crack!

"You've got a great ass."

Crack!

"It jiggles like a big bowl of Jell-O."

Crack!

"You getting hot, slut? Your ass is practically glowing."

Christ! The stroke drove her down onto the poorly padded surface of what served as a spanking bench, but in reality, was nothing more than a board with a far too thin layer of cheap foam, covered by a piece of faux leather.

Crack!

"Why so quiet, is this not doing it for you?"

Crack!

"Perhaps a cane would get a response out of you. Is that what you need, baby?"

Not unless you want me to shove it where the sun doesn't shine. Of course, she couldn't actually voice her true feelings. Instead, Charlize gave the requisite moan of bliss the man wielding the wooden paddle expected.

"That's better, baby. I knew you were enjoying this."

Crack!

You don't know shit about me! Another drawn out moan, another tantalizing swish of her hips given as she planned her speech for when she accepted her Oscar for best actress in a fucked-up role.

Giving another moan, without the benefit of any writhing of supposed arousal this time, she lifted her head to scan what she could see of her surroundings.

Shit, where the fuck is he? He should have been here by now. I'm going to beat someone to a bloody pulp...

Charlize was jerked from her thoughts of retribution when she realized two things. The blows had stopped and the cheeks of her burning ass were being ripped apart.

4

What the fuck! She considered herself someone who went above and beyond the requirements of her job, but enough was enough.

"No!"

One cheek was released as a searing strike to its surface was given. "You don't give the orders. Your job is to take whatever you're given." The hand reclaimed her buttock, rough fingers digging into hot flesh. "As much pleasure as I got paddling your ass, it's my turn for some fun."

"Get off!"

His response to her order was to chuckle. "Oh, don't worry. I'm going to be getting off."

Forget it. She'd never agreed to this! Releasing the leather straps she'd been pulling against, she attempted to twist around as she shouted, "Red!"

The breath whooshed out of her as he pressed his knee into the small of her back to keep her pinned to the bench. "Is that supposed to be a safeword?" He fisted her hair, pulling her head back so far her neck felt as if it would snap. She tried not to retch as his sour breath wafted over her when he leaned down. "Where do you think you are? Some fancy club with chicken-shit rules? Well, darling, consider this as *my* club and there are no fucking rules."

Charlize discovered where his other hand had gone when she felt it pawing between her legs. This time, it was his turn to curse as his fingers dug painfully into her sex. "Fuck! What the hell? You're dry as the fucking desert." The first genuine cry of pain she'd given came as he gripped the lips of her pussy and twisted hard.

"I bought your ass so shut the fuck up and enjoy the ride."

Her sex continued to throb even with his hand's disappearance. She heard the unmistakable sound of a zipper being lowered as her hair was yanked again, forcing her to turn her head. She didn't bother glancing at the cock he had dug from the confines of his jeans to run his free hand lewdly up and down its length. Instead, her attention was focused on the appearance of her contact as he shook the hand of the man who served as Sorenson's accountant. Finally, after working for months, it was time to take this asshole and his organization down.

"Alamo!" she screamed.

"That's right. I don't need you wet. Just like Santa Anna, I'm gonna be fucking a Texan up the ass, and you're gonna beg for..."

His words were cut off when hoards of people poured inside, all shouting orders as chaos erupted. "What the fuck!" he shouted, jumping off of her.

Pushing up, Charlize said, "You're under arrest..." Her next sound was one of pain as she was yanked off the bench by her hair and a fist connected with her midsection.

"You're a fucking cop!" As he roared, he bent forward and Charlize knew his goal the moment she saw the knife he'd tucked back into his boot after cutting her clothes off, coming free. Ignoring both the agonizing pull on her hair and the throbbing in her stomach, she didn't think—just reacted.

With a high kick, she knocked the knife from his hand and grabbed his arm. In another blur of movement, she flipped him over her shoulder. She had to hand it to the bastard—despite the thudding impact as he slammed into the floor, his erection still jutted from his pants.

The sound of several guns cocking didn't draw his eyes to the agents aiming them at him. Instead, his eyes were locked on Charlize's foot that she'd placed on his groin, the five-inch black stiletto heel a bare inch from his quickly deflating cock as she continued to list his crimes as if nothing had happened. "For the possession of illegal drugs with the intent to sell, solicitation, resisting arrest—"

"Get the fuck off me, bitch!"

Charlize rocked her foot back just a bit as she 'adjusted' her stance.

His eyes widened, but only for an instant, quickly filling with a look of pure hatred. "Do you know who the hell I am? You can't come in here and—"

"Assault of a federal officer, attempted murder of that same officer and, well, for just being the sleaziest asshole on the face of the planet." Fighting the impulse to really grind the heel into his flesh, Charlize recited the Miranda warning, lifted her foot and said, "Get him out of here."

Sorenson was dragged to his feet and his hands quickly secured behind him with a plastic zip-tie.

"You're making a huge mistake. The governor is a personal friend of mine. By the time my lawyers get through with you, you'll be nothing but a meter maid," Sorenson snarled.

"I don't give a shit if the governor is your bosom buddy," Charlize said, stepping closer. "Perhaps your fancy lawyers can explain since you obviously weren't listening. I said *federal officer*. I'm not a cop, I am a DEA agent, dickhead." For the first time since the task force had stormed into the mansion, Robert Sorenson's eyes widened and his mouth opened and closed without words or threats making their way past his shock. Charlize shook her head, turned away and then turned back. "And for God's sake, will someone please tuck that pathetic excuse for a dick away?"

"Shit, are you all right?"

Charlize turned to see Dillon MacAllister, the FBI liaison on the joint-task force. "I'm fine."

"Why the fuck did you take so long to code? You could have been killed!"

"Well, I wasn't and I had to make sure we had enough to put his ass away for good."

"Still—"

"My call," Charlize said, turning to see Dillon's eyes flashing. When his mouth opened, she shook her head. "We'll discuss it later, when this is over. For now..." A shout caused her to whip around in time to see Alejandro Cortez haul off and slug the agent

7

who was attempting to cuff him. The scuffle ended in an exchange of blows and by the time it was over, Alejandro was not only cuffed, his suit was torn and his nose broken. Sorenson, his accountant, and the other men already cuffed and lined up against the wall witnessed him being hauled off by the INS, assuring that the others would think he'd been taken to a different facility for processing. Yes, the undercover cop definitely deserved an Oscar for best actor in what they all were expecting to be the biggest drug bust in Texas history.

Charlize then took note of the women standing with eyes wide in various states of undress. Though she was pretty positive the women weren't guilty of anything worse than wanting a chance to have a better life, this wasn't the way to go about it.

"Carson, take everyone in... Carson!"

"What?" A rookie agent's head snapped up, a flush staining his cheeks as she just stared at him. "Sorry, sir... I mean ma'am... I mean—"

"Take the women too."

"The women?"

"Oh for Christ's sake," Charlize said, sweeping her hand to point out the women in the room. "Yes, the women. The ICE is going to want to talk to every one of them. I'm sure they'll find some aren't here legally. They can sort it out at the station."

The agent looked grateful to have been given a task and turned away.

Addressing Dillon, she asked, "Do you have the warrants?"

"Yes—"

"Then let's tear the place apart, shall we?" She didn't wait for a response, beginning to walk towards the door the agents had stormed through.

"Hey, wait up."

Charlize didn't stop walking, and made it almost to the door before a hand on her shoulder held her in place. Whirling, her leg had already come up, knee bent, heel ready to snap forward when Dillon stepped back, lifting his hands, palms out.

"Whoa! Shit, take it easy. I just figured you might want to put some clothes on first."

* * *

SHIT! No wonder the rookie hadn't been listening. She'd totally forgotten she was naked.

"Charlie?"

Dillon's soft call of her nickname snapped her out of her memory. Shrugging, she confessed, "I'm afraid my clothes didn't survive."

The concern morphed into fury and she saw his eyes flick to the wall where Sorenson had been placed. "Fuck!"

"Don't worry, he didn't get that far," Charlize said, attempting to lighten the mood.

"Not funny," Dillon said, his expression darkening as his eyes raked down her torso. "Fuck," he said again as he shrugged out of his vest with FBI emblazoned in large yellow letters across the back. After dropping it to the floor, he pulled his t-shirt over his head.

"Here."

She reached for it only to find that he'd already bunched the material up and was holding it, ready for her to stick her head into the neck opening. Was he so disgusted by the bruises that were already blooming on her body that he couldn't wait to cover them up? Instead of allowing him to help, she yanked the shirt out of his hands. "Thanks, I've got it." What had been molded to a muscular body hung loosely on her, but she didn't care. The hem came to mid-thigh. Hell, the shirt offered more coverage than the dress she'd worn into the club. Charlie looked up to see his eyes had softened.

"You did good, you know."

Meeting his eyes, she finally took a breath that didn't feel as if it took supreme effort, but she had more work to do. "It's my job and it's not finished, are you ready?"

"You've done enough. We'll take it from here. Why don't you go on home—"

"No! I'm not leaving until it's over. I've worked too hard..." Afraid her voice would crack, she paused. If she wanted to be able to look the only people in the room who mattered in the eyes again—those men and women with whom she'd formed even a temporary bond—she couldn't leave. "Come on, we've got a job to do."

"You're right," Dillon interrupted. "This is your bust. Let me get Lucy and we'll start."

Charlize got through the next several hours solely by concentrating on her job. Various people came and went but she remained, issuing orders, directing teams, witnessing the search authorized by warrants being executed by teams of agents and their partners, resulting in the discovery of more drugs and money than they'd even expected.

"Shit, I've seen a lot of busts, but this is unbelievable," Dillon said as the last panel was removed. Stacks of white bricks were lined up behind a false wall in one of the outlying buildings. Another building held a lab where the cocaine was cut and packaged to be sold after being smuggled in from Mexico. They'd also confiscated enough neatly packaged currency to have paid for the property a hundred times over, including the money the undercover officer Cortez had turned over in exchange for becoming the group's newest partner. Hundreds of head of cattle grazed in the surrounding fields, a perfect cover for what was, in reality, a huge drug running operation in Brownsville, Texas, practically spitting distance from Mexico.

It was another two hours before she and Dillon left the ranch, and when they walked into the station, it was to see Captain James Morrow's eyes widening at the sight of the FBI special agent's bare chest beneath his vest and a DEA agent dressed in nothing but a t-shirt and high heels.

"What the hell happened to your clothes?"

Charlize shrugged. "It was a sex party, Captain. Debriefing in the conference room, right?"

"Not looking like that, you don't. Go change, Fullerton."

"Yes, sir," she said, changing direction and heading the opposite way. Opening the metal door of a locker, she pulled on the clothes she'd shed so many hours ago. She couldn't bring herself to strip and shower, telling herself that the others were waiting. Entering the conference room, she accepted a mug of coffee from Officer Cortez.

"Thanks, how's your nose?"

"Fine, look, I'm sorry it took so long, Charlie... they counted and checked every single bill or else I'd have been done before you had to—"

"Don't worry about it. We got them," Charlie said, cutting him off and pulling out a chair to join those already seated around the table.

Hours passed as the personnel making up the task force went over every step of the sting from the moment she'd entered the house until the moment she'd arrived at the station.

"So that's that," Morrow said, the chair creaking beneath his weight as he leaned back. "This is the largest drug bust we've ever had." Meeting Charlize's eyes, he said, "You were right; all but two of the women had been smuggled across the border. Most paid all they had for the promise of a green card and a job. None expected the job to be as... um... escorts. You did good, Agent Fullerton. Sorenson's gang will be unlikely to see the light of day for the next century or so. We've finally got them."

"The team did good," she countered. Looking around the table, she continued. "It took months and the cooperation of the FBI, DEA, ICE, and local law enforcement, but yeah, we got them."

The door opened and Stephanie Hiller walked in. The fact that the district attorney wasn't smiling telegraphed that the team wouldn't be allowed to bask in the captain's praise for long. "We've got a problem."

When she didn't elaborate, Morrow leaned forward again. "Are we supposed to play twenty fucking questions? Spit it out."

"Sorenson is calling foul. He's claiming entrapment and states he was assaulted by Agent Fullerton. That she had a knife and tried to stab—"

"That's bullshit," Cortez said. "Where in the hell would she get a knife? She was buck ass naked for God's sake!"

Charlize appreciated his coming instantly to her defense, but could have done without the disclosure of her lack of attire. Not only the captain and the district attorney, but even the stenographer taking notes looked in her direction. She did notice that the task force members were making it a point to look elsewhere.

"That true?" Morrow asked.

"That I was nude—"

The captain waved his hand. "Not that part. The part about entrapment."

"Absolutely not, I'm not some fucking rookie." She glared at the district attorney. "You can't possibly believe him. He's just fishing."

Hiller slid into the chair opposite Charlize. "I'm on your side here." After Charlize nodded, she continued, "He states he specifically asked if you were a cop before... engaging you, and that you lied."

Charlize's exhaustion didn't keep her anger at bay. Locking her eyes with the district attorney, she stated in a cold voice. "He asked and I evaded. He then took *his* knife and cut my clothes off looking for a wire."

"Do you remember if anyone was around who could validate your answer?"

"Oh, for Pete's sake, if Charlie states she didn't lie, then she didn't," Dillon said, exasperation evident in his tone.

"Look, I'm just telling you what Sorenson is going to be claiming to his lawyers, so how about doing us all a favor and stop shooting the messenger, okay? Were you in the room to witness the exchange, Special Agent MacAllister?"

"Fuck, if I'd been in the room, there would never have been an *exchange.*"

"Exactly my point. So, unless one of Sorenson's guests disputes his claim, then, like I said, it could be a problem. Not an insurmountable one as Agent Fullerton's record will be considered."

Charlie saw Dillon's jaw clench "It's all right. I don't need anyone to validate my story," she said, unfastening the band of the watch on her wrist and flipping it across the table. "Check the tape. I didn't lie and I didn't assault the shithead. I defended myself. The man's a criminal. You can't be surprised to discover he's a lying sonofabitch as well."

Stephanie looked at the watch and then grinned. "So not totally naked, huh? Good for you for remembering to accessorize. I've heard of these, but haven't seen one. Please tell me they really work."

Charlize's anger slipped away as she understood the woman was just doing her job and was now attempting to defuse the tension. "Let's just say that by the time you've got the recording transcribed, you'll have no doubt that Sorenson's hook came back empty."

"It's my biggest dream to slam the door on his cage and throw away the damn key," Hiller said.

Charlize knew they all felt the same. Sorenson's operation had run drugs and human beings across the border for years. He'd always hidden behind his ranch, his family name, his political connections. But this time, after months of blood, sweat, and tears, they had him. She turned to the captain. "Are we about done here?"

"Yes," Captain Morrow said after glancing at the sunlight streaming through the cheap venetian blinds at the window. "Go home and get some rest. It'll take weeks to sort through all this shit, but for now, it can wait. Good job everyone."

* * *

DAWN HAD long come and gone by the time Charlize stepped out of the station. Despite the blazing heat, she shuddered.

"Come on, I'll treat you to breakfast," Dillon said, reaching out to take her arm, dropping his hand when she flinched. "Hey, you okay, Charlie?"

"I'm fine—"

"So you do lie," he countered.

"What?"

"It's just me, Charlie. No team, no captain, no DA. You're not fine. You are shaking..." When she opened her mouth, he shook his head. "What you did tonight was incredible, but it also had a high price. A check you picked up by yourself. It's all right to be shaken. And don't bother to tell me you aren't. It's probably ninety degrees out here already, and yet you've got that blazer buttoned all the way. I just want you to know that I'm here if you need to talk or just to listen if you want to scream, or hell, I'll even take a few punches if you want to hit something."

She saw the concern reflected in his eyes. "I know. Thanks for having my back, at the ranch and in there," she said, nodding to indicate the building behind them.

"That's what partners do," he said, brushing off her thanks.

Charlize knew that they weren't technically partners, but appreciated the sentiment. "Thanks again for the offer, but I'm afraid I'd do a face plant into my pancakes."

"Yeah, you do look beat. Look, let me drive you home. You can pick up your car tomorrow."

"Thanks, but no. You go on. You know how Lucy is. She won't actually believe you are fine until she sees you."

"Are you sure?"

"Yes, I'll be fine. Give her a hug for me. She and the others did an amazing job. I'm going to fall into bed and just sleep." They continued towards the parking lot where he waited until she slid into her Tahoe before giving a wave and moving to his rental car. Charlize knew she'd just lied to him. She had no intention of falling into bed... well, not yet. She'd not be able to sleep until she scrubbed every single inch of her skin. From the moment Sorenson had touched her, she'd felt dirty. No, she corrected herself. Not dirty... filthy. Even if the bastard hadn't destroyed her clothes, she never would have worn them again.

CHAPTER 2

*H*er fingers were trembling as she unbuttoned the navy blue blazer. It took far too long to slip the buttons from the buttonholes down the front of her white blouse and to peel out of the navy blue pants. For the first time, the ensemble she considered her official 'uniform', hadn't made her feel proud, and somehow Dillon had known that. By the time Charlize actually got into her bath, tired had been replaced by utter exhaustion. Groaning, she sank into the steaming water and reached for the loofah. Not allowing the tenderness caused by the paddling to stop her, she soaped and scrubbed repeatedly, not setting it aside until every inch of her skin was red. Not trusting her legs to support her, she turned the water on again and reached for the hand-held shower unit. She flinched a bit as the stream hit her head, but gritted her teeth and washed her hair. Pulling the plug, she watched the small funnel appear as the water drained. With every inch that lowered in the tub, she told herself that the filth she'd felt at Sorenson's touch was being sucked away, but was afraid she was only attempting to fool herself.

Using her hands to push up, she couldn't contain a soft groan the motion required to stand. For a woman in great physical condition, she suddenly felt like an old lady—brittle, weak, fragile.

"Stop it!" she chastised. "You're supposed to be stronger than this."

Stepping over the rim of the bathtub, she grabbed a towel and began to dry off. Catching a glimpse of her reflection in the mirror on the back of the door, she froze. Bruises had bloomed on her breasts from where Sorenson had mauled her. The hand in the mirror lifted and moved towards a nipple and the woman standing alone and naked winced at the gentle touch. Turning slightly, she saw that her ass was also bruised and the image in the mirror shifted.

"Why do you use your hand first?"

"Any good dominant knows that it's important to take the time to warm his submissive slowly, to allow the blood to come to the surface. I don't want you to bruise... well, not easily, and not with the first stroke."

She'd felt a delicious shiver of anticipation run through as he had continued to place swats all across the surface of her ass.

Lifting her head and looking over her shoulder, she'd smiled. "Hmm, that sounds a bit too convenient... for the Dom that is."

Charlize had indeed felt warmth flooding through her when he'd grinned. "Believe me, it's for your own good." When she rolled her eyes, he had chuckled. "And, young lady, you'll learn that a submissive rolling her eyes is apt to earn herself extra strokes."

She'd still not been able to hold back her smile as she'd relaxed over his lap. For the first time in her life, she had felt that it was all right to enjoy kink, to let herself trust someone to take her to places she'd always dreamed about, but never explored. She worked so hard, pushed herself to the limit in a world demanding perfection, her shoulders bent beneath the weight of responsibility and proving that a woman could handle the job of a DEA agent. But that night, in the safety of the club, she could just be Charlie—a woman who craved to submit to someone. To no longer be tough, to be soft and pliant under a dominant's hand.

"Good girl," he'd said, as he sat back and resumed his 'warm up' that

felt suspiciously like a spanking to her—granted, a very sexy spanking— but nonetheless, a spanking. By the time the dominant guided her off his lap and led her to the St. Andrew's cross, she still wasn't sure his story held any truth, but was absolutely positive that she was burning and eager to take their play to a much deeper level.

A soft moan snapped her out of the memory. What the hell? She'd honestly believed she would do her job and come out of it unscathed. It wasn't like she'd never played before—didn't know what to expect. But, instead of the rush, the pleasure she always experienced playing at a club, the flushed skin, the bright eyes, she... Looking up, the mirror showed a woman whose eyes were filled with pain... and not from the bruises that decorated her body. Forcing herself not to drop her eyes, to face her reflection head on, she said, "Sorenson isn't a dominant... he's a fucking sadist. A criminal. And you aren't his submissive so stop trying to convince yourself this was just a trip to a club for a little kinky R&R. It was just a job. Forget it and move on."

She tightened the towel around her torso, tucking the ends together above her breasts. She'd only managed to begin to comb out her wet hair when the pull of its teeth caused her to gasp. Forcing back the tears she could feel threatening to well at the pain from having her hair not only pulled, but actual strands ripped from her scalp, she slammed the comb onto the counter and fled the room and its mirrors that revealed too much.

The trill of her cellphone split the silence.

"God, I can't... please just let me sleep," she said, returning to the bathroom to dig the phone from the pocket of her blazer, only to have it stop ringing.

Sighing, she retraced her steps, set the phone on the night-stand and pulled back the bedspread. She was so exhausted; she was swaying on her feet. Too tired to even think, she dropped the towel and slid between the sheets. She'd just closed her eyes when a tone again sounded signaling she'd received a text message.

"I swear to God, if you tell me to come back in, I'm going to shoot someone!" Pulling the phone to her, she swept her finger over the message icon.

Just wanted to say I'm proud of you. You're one hell of an agent. Oh, and Lucy sends her love. Good night, Charlie.

It was just a note from one agent to another and yet, Charlie felt her eyes well. The shame that had flooded her in the bathroom, the knowledge that Dillon had seen her naked, bruised, and the fear that he judged her had only added to that shame. And yet, the simple text and words of praise pushed some of the shame away. Her fingers flew to answer.

I needed that. Tell Lucy she's a very lucky lady to have you for her partner. Good night, Dillon, and thanks.

* * *

Two Weeks Later

"So, where do you go from here?"

Popping the tortilla chip she'd just loaded with salsa into her mouth, Charlie chewed and swallowed before answering.

"Believe it or not, I'm being forced to take vacation."

"Shit, Charlie, you make it sound like you expect to be tortured."

"Very funny," she said, another chip already dipped into the bowl as she shook her head and looked across the table at Dillon. "Seriously though, I don't think I even know what that word means anymore. What do people actually do on vacation?"

"It depends on what you're into. You can either sign-up for some adventure..." He paused as he moved out of the booth to stand.

"What's wrong?" Surprised at his abrupt movement, she turned to look behind her and saw a man approaching. Leaving the chip in the salsa, she scooted to the edge of the bench and had just made it to her feet when Captain Morrow arrived.

"Fullerton, do you ever wear an actual uniform?"

Charlize glanced down at her clothing which consisted of an A&M sweatshirt, a pair of jeans that had holes at the knees and her favorite pair of sneakers. Looking back at the captain, she said, "Don't tell me; you're a University of Texas man?" She reached for the cloth napkin on the table and tucked it into the neckline of her sweatshirt, covering up the large "Gig Em Aggies" logo. Smoothing it down with her fingers, she looked up. "Better?"

The captain rolled his eyes, but Charlize saw his lips twitch as he shook his head. "You're a smartass, Fullerton." He paused and held out his hand. "You're also one hell of a cop. I just wanted to stop by and say thank you. You're both welcome to come back anytime."

Charlize was touched. Ignoring his extended hand, she stepped closer, lifting up onto her toes and buzzed his cheek with her lips. "Thanks, Captain. You run a good ship."

His face flushed, but his eyes twinkled as she stepped back. "You made a believer out of me. Even with all the goddamn red tape, combined agencies are the way to go if we're ever going to win the war against drugs and smuggling. You take care of yourself, Charlize."

"I will, sir." She watched as he made his way towards the door, laughing when he lifted his hand over his head, giving her the 'Hook'em Horns' sign. Slipping back into the booth, she said, "Wow, that was unexpected."

"What? That he is a UT fan or that he wanted to express his appreciation?" Dillon asked, taking his seat and picking up his bottle of beer. "The man may be a little rough, but he's a good guy."

Charlize shook her head, and lifted her glass. "I know he's a good guy. I just didn't think he actually knew my first name."

Dillon chuckled. "He's right, you know. You are a smartass."

Flapping her hand, she said, "So, go on. You were giving me the definition of vacation. So, adventure, huh?"

He shook his head. "You know what? I think you've had enough adventure for a while. Hell, you've not only got balls of steel, you have skills I've never seen. When you flipped Sorenson to his back and stood there totally nake—" Charlize watched as he paused and he took another long swallow of his beer. "I just meant that with your foot on his gut, you looked like some big game trophy hunter. I think you can check adventure off your bucket list."

"Good save," she said, "even though I don't consider weasels as trophy material. So, what does that leave?"

"Relax—"

"Any more relaxed and you're going to have to pour me into my car." She laughed and held up her frosted mug.

Dillon shook his head. "I mean on your vacation. Don't even think about work, don't train, don't read manuals... just be a girl."

Charlie smiled. "In case you haven't noticed, MacAllister, I am a girl."

"A smartass girl," he said. "I'm serious. Go shopping for shit you don't really need. Get your hair and nails done. Hell, go to a spa and let someone pamper you for a change. You're damn good at your job, but how about giving just being Charlize a chance? I know that beneath that tough exterior is a rose—a yellow rose—just dying to bloom."

She didn't just spout out some snarky remark. His low tone, the look in his eyes, was doing something to her insides. "Wow, so how in the hell did she get to you, huh?"

"What? Who?"

"Martha." She laughed as it was obvious he was at a total loss. "Never mind. It's just that when you said all that about relaxing, I couldn't help but think you'd spoken to Martha. She was my college roommate, and actually, I'm going to spend part of my vacation with her. She is the poster woman for all that 'girly' stuff."

"Good. You deserve to have some fun. Get all dolled up and go strut your stuff. Go dancing, just don't flip the guy over your shoulder when he holds you during some slow song. We're not all misogynists, you know. Some of us actually know how to treat a lady." His expression changed as his lips curled and his eyes darkened.

When her stomach fluttered again, she set down her margarita, her hand a bit shaky.

"You okay?"

"Brain freeze," she said, not about to admit that she'd just felt a pull that had been missing from her life for so long.

"Let's order," he said, signaling for the waitress. "You're tough as shit but you're a skinny little thing. No more margaritas for you. You need some food to counter that tequila."

Charlize pulled her mug to her chest as he reached for it. "No way. I'm on vacation, remember?" As if to emphasize her statement, she sucked down the last of the glass's contents in one long slurp, giving a long moan of appreciation.

"You're the only person I know who moans like that," Dillon said, lifting his beer bottle to his lips.

Charlize swallowed, shaking her head. "God, that's just so sad, MacAllister."

Dillon lowered his bottle and gave her a puzzled look then chuckled. "Walked right into that one, didn't I?"

"Hook, line, and sinker," Charlie teased, reaching for the menu, but looking at him instead. "If you'll buy me another margarita, I can give you a list of books, or heck, even some videos that could help you with that problem."

"How very generous of you," he interjected. "But that won't be necessary."

Closing the menu as she knew she'd be ordering the same thing she always did, ever since Dillon had first brought her to the small hole-in-the-wall restaurant, she sat back and smiled. "Whew, good to know. For a moment there, I thought I was gonna learn that you were lacking in some very vital skills."

A dimple appeared in his cheek as he bent forward to whisper, "Don't you fret, little one. I graduated with top honors in the course Fabulous Bedroom Interactions. That's the part of the training we take to make us *Special* FBI Agents."

She laughed and rolled her eyes. "You are so full of shit, MacAllister."

"Shut up and order, Fullerton."

They enjoyed their meal, and he did buy her a second margarita. Charlie knew she was really going to miss some of the best conversation she'd ever had as well as the most authentic Tex-Mex food she'd ever eaten. Picking up the last sopapilla in the basket, she dipped it in the bowl of warm honey, closing her eyes in bliss as the crisply fried dough melted on her tongue. When she opened them again, she found Dillon staring at her, an expression on his face that she hadn't seen before.

"What?"

He reached across the table and touched his fingertip to the corner of her mouth, and a bolt of electricity shot straight through her. When he withdrew it, a drop of honey glistening on his fingertip, and his tongue flicked to lick the sweetness, she was instantly thrown back several months to the night he'd caught her by surprise and kissed her. She was suddenly very sorry she'd stepped away even though her heart had started to pound the moment his lips touched hers. She was even sorrier that when he'd not given up and had asked her out, she turned him down. Knowing they needed to focus on the operation, their research turning up the fact that the ranch hosted these sex parties, she'd had a suspicion she'd be going undercover. Once again, she'd set aside her personal wishes and insisted they keep their relationship professional... and strictly platonic. Now, she was having regrets... big time.

"I was just thinking, I'm really gonna miss you," Dillon said.

Charlize was about to lift her finger to lick the last of the honey off, but stuck it in her water glass instead, wiping it clean with her napkin, blushing when he just grinned. "No, you're not. I've been nothing but a burr under your saddle since I got here. Admit it, the captain wasn't exactly thrilled to discover he'd be forced to include a female DEA Agent in his little club. Big tough FBI and ICE agents, yeah, they are automatic members. But a female agent? Nope, not so much. Don't think I don't know how many times you stood up for me when he was bitching."

Dillon gave a self-deprecating grin. "Well, you heard him. Captain Morrow may be old-school, but he admitted you taught him a thing or two about how very effective women are when given the chance. Hell, you've got more balls than most men I know." When she lifted her margarita glass, he clicked his bottle of Corona against it in a toast. "And nobody can deny that you've kept it interesting." Swallowing the last of his beer, he shook his head. "Promise me something, Charlie."

"I'm not a big believer in promises," she said, then saw the question in his eyes. Instead of answering, she took another sip of her drink and added, "But, go ahead and ask. If I can, I'll do my best to try."

"I mean it, Charlie, you keep at it and one day you're going to wake up and realize that you're old and life has passed you by. There is more to life than your job."

"The job is who I am," Charlie said, wondering how their cele-bration had turned into a discussion she didn't particularly want to have.

"No," Dillon said, shaking his head. "It's what you do. Granted, you're one of the toughest people I know, but, fuck, Charlie, you've got to step away and take a good long look at yourself. Is this really what you want?"

Charlize knew she could have blown him off, could have lied or flat out told him to put a lid on it, but she'd come to think of

Dillon as a friend. They'd worked side by side for months, shared many a meal, and she was honest enough to say that while she thought Lucy was great, she was also jealous of her. "I've worked very hard to get where I am. I'm happy."

"Bullshit."

Her head snapped up from where she'd been looking down into her drink, a little shocked at the vehemence of his tone. "How about we just cut the therapy session?"

"How is that vow of solitude working out for you?"

She slammed down the mug she'd just emptied. "What the fuck, Dillon? You don't have the right to judge me. Hell, you don't even know me!"

"I know enough, and even if you want to throw it back in my face, I care enough about you to be honest. Yes, you've worked your ass off. Yes, you've had to deal with a bunch of assholes who think women should be kept barefoot and pregnant and preferably in the kitchen. You've had to fight for the right to be given the opportunities that most men are simply handed. But, tell me, Charlie, and for fuck's sake, be honest for once... tell me, is that all you want in life? To go it all alone? Too scared of being seen as a female to actually enjoy being one?"

"Don't! You have no idea what it's like to be a woman in a man's world. When you have to struggle for every damn thing!"

"Wrong, I do. And do you know how? Because I've worked with a great many female agents. And, Charlie, not all of them are as determined to prove they have a set of balls swinging between their legs as you are. They find a way to balance the job and allow themselves to find joy in living a life outside the damn job. Hell, you're whining about being forced to take a vacation."

"When's the last time you had a vacation? Huh? You work as hard as I do, and yet... yet you act like I- I... I don't know, like I'm a freak or something."

Dillon sat back and sighed. "That's not what I was saying and you know it. I'm just saying give yourself a chance to see the things I see. Don't only be proud that you're a great agent, be proud that you're an intelligent, beautiful—"

"Girl? Is that what you want? For me to wear dresses and high heels? The last time I did was the same night I had a knife put to my throat. It was a damn good thing I could take care of myself then and I can take care of myself now."

Dillon leaned closer, his eyes dark as molten chocolate. "You aren't listening to what I'm saying." When her mouth opened, he shook his head, reached across and put his fingertip on her lips. "Enough. All I'm saying is that you don't have to go it alone, Charlie. Let someone—"

She jerked her head back. "What? Park their ass in my living room where they'll fart, belch, and scratch their balls while I bring them beers and cook their dinner? Is that what you really want?"

If anything, he leaned even closer. "No, damn it! What I'm saying is I should have followed my gut and given you what you needed that night. I should have—"

"What? Turned me over your knee and taken your turn at beating my ass?" She could hear herself almost cackling but couldn't seem to stop. "Well, hell, Dillon, you missed a great opportunity. You wouldn't have even had to yank my panties down as I was already —how did Cortez put it—oh, yeah, buck ass naked!" She could feel her heart racing and the fact that she was having trouble drawing in enough air had it taking a moment before she realized the gasp she heard hadn't come from her.

Turning her head, Charlize saw that diners at nearby booths had stopped dipping chips into bowls of salsa to stare over and listen. She'd long thought she'd become immune to what others thought, but that was no excuse to be shouting in a restaurant where families with children were enjoying dinner out.

"Oh, God, I- I'm sorry," she said, embarrassment over her behavior causing her to bury her face in her hands... a face that felt like it had a third degree sunburn.

Dillon reached across and pulled her hands away from her

face, holding them in his. "No, Charlize. I should have pulled you into my arms and held you. I should have told you that I knew how scared you were despite the bravado you hide behind. Instead, I let you hurt—"

"Don't," she said softly, fighting back tears that threatened to fall. "You were the only one who even asked if I was all right." Looking across the table, she saw Dillon in a new light. Somehow he understood that she wasn't anywhere near as tough as she appeared. That the persona she projected, one she'd worked so hard to attain, was nothing but a tough exterior protecting the true woman inside. "I- I volunteered. I knew going in what was likely to happen. Hell, I prepared for it for months when we discovered that they threw those parties. But... but you called and sent a text. That allowed me to forgive myself."

"Fuck, Charlie, you have nothing to forgive yourself for..." When she opened her mouth to protest, he again touched her lips with a fingertip. "And, young lady, if you dare say one smartass word in argument, I will be flipping you over my knees."

"You and what army?" she asked, unable to stop herself.

"Okay, I'll let that one go, smartass," he said with a grin. "I deserve that for not stepping up when you needed me. But, I am serious. You deserve better. Promise me that you'll take this chance to start over. To build a life you'll actually enjoy existing in —not just watch the days come and go."

She didn't pull her hand away, didn't instantly pop off with some smartass remark. What she did do was wonder if perhaps he was right... not about being deserving. Hell, she wasn't any more deserving than the next guy, but maybe Dillon was right that it was time to make some changes.

"I'll promise I'll try."

He gave her fingers a squeeze and then lifted his hand. "That's all I ask. How about some coffee?"

"No, I've got to finish packing and get some sleep. I've got a long drive so need to get on the road early tomorrow, but, thanks,

Dillon. Despite the therapy session, it really was a pleasure working with you. I mean that."

Dillon motioned to the waitress for the check. Once the tab was paid, he walked her out to her Tahoe and when she pressed the fob to unlock it, he pulled the door open. When she turned and extended her hand, he ignored it, pulling her into a hug. "The pleasure is all mine, Charlie. If you're ever in need of back-up, just give me a call."

"Thanks again, Dillon. I really am going to miss you." As she had done with Captain Morrow, she lifted up and kissed his cheek, wishing she had the guts to kiss him as she suddenly yearned to do. To pull his lips to hers, to show him she was sorry she'd not given them a chance to become more than friends. To cover the emotion that thought had caused, she said, "You do have something in common with the captain you know."

"How come I think you're going to disparage my honor and call me a chauvinistic pig?" Dillon asked.

"And insult some poor sweet little piggy?" Charlie said, her hand over her heart. "Not at all. But, you are both a bit old-school and bossy... hey! What was that for?" she asked, her hand moving to her ass to rub the spot he'd just popped.

"If I took the time to tell you all the reasons, well, darlin', I'm afraid you'd find your vacation was over before it began." He smiled and lifted her chin with his fingertip and bent down to kiss her softly. Straightening, he said, "Drive carefully and take care of yourself, Charlize. And when you walk onto that field, know that I'm there in the stadium, proud as hell to be your twelfth man."

Memories of standing in the bleachers at Kyle Field, screaming for her team, one of thousands of fans who all represented that one person—that twelfth man—never sitting down in a show of support, had been some of the best days of her life, and she so appreciated Dillon stating he was her fan and yet she was fighting back tears as she slipped behind the wheel. Looking up, she said, "You're a good man, Special Agent MacAllister." He smiled and shut her door and she pulled out. Turning right, knowing he'd be turning left, she watched in her rearview mirror as his taillights disappeared. Only then did she pull around the corner and to the curb. She couldn't see for the tears in her eyes. Charlie felt her heart stutter in her chest as she felt the promise of what might have been and realized she'd been a fool. Yes, they'd partnered together, had taken down a drug ring but at what cost? She'd not taken a chance to discover what they might have found together. Not as agents, but as a man and a woman. And now... now it was too late.

CHAPTER 3

"Oh my God! You're finally here!" Martha said as she yanked the door open and practically pulled Charlie out from behind the wheel, wrapping her arms around her. "Next time how about taking a plane? I mean, who drives across country anymore? I could have picked you up at the airport."

Charlie laughed and hugged her right back. "I actually enjoy the drive and I really didn't want to put you out—"

"Are you out of your ever freaking mind? I've been begging you to get your ass to D.C. for years," Martha said, pulling Charlie's suitcase from the Tahoe. "Hurry up. Grab your shit and let's get inside."

Charlie grinned, pulling the strap of her duffle over her shoulder. "What? Embarrassed to be seen with me?"

Martha smiled as she closed the door after getting Charlie's laptop bag. "Of course not. But we've got a lot of catching up to do and…" she paused, her head swiveling as she looked around. Evidently satisfied, she said, "And what I've got to tell you is gonna blow your socks off."

"Don't tell me, you've discovered some big loophole in the tax law," Charlie teased as the two women entered the townhouse.

"I said blow your socks off, not put you into a coma," Martha retorted. "Though, you would be surprised at how interesting taxes can be."

"No, I'd be stunned," Charlie said, following her old college roommate up the stairs.

"Ha-ha, very funny. You're in here." Martha opened the door and led the way inside. "It's not much, but at least it's bigger than our dorm room was."

Charlie looked around. There was an antique white, iron bed with beautiful metal work of vines and leaves at the head and foot of the bed. A dresser that had been painted white and then distressed to look a bit battered sat against one wall. A sturdy oak table that reminded Charlie of those she'd sat at in many a library served as a desk and was placed beneath a window where white lacy curtains hung. A thick blue rug covered a large portion of the hardwood floors, and a vase of fresh flowers stood on the night-stand. Charlie set her duffel on top of the patchwork quilt that covered the bed.

"It's lovely," she said, then grinned. "God, it really is good to see you."

The two women embraced. The first time they'd met had been in a dorm room. They both showed up that first day as freshmen at Texas A&M, to discover that they were roomies. That was the day they began a friendship that graduation, separate career paths, and moves across country hadn't weakened. After Charlie released her, Martha said. "I'm glad you like it. The bathroom is across the hall and my room is at the end. Go ahead and unpack and freshen up, then come downstairs. I've got chili in the crockpot and cornbread ready to go into the oven."

"Your famous cornbread? With the actual corn niblets, cheese, and jalapeños?" Charlie asked, her mouth already watering.

"Of course. Why bother making it if it's not Mexican corn-bread? Oh, and a bottle of wine that we won't have to dilute with soda in order to drink it."

Charlie laughed, remembering countless bottles of cheap wine they'd shared. "Sounds wonderful. I don't have much to unpack, so I'll be down in just a few."

Once Martha left, Charlie emptied the contents of her duffel into the top two drawers of the dresser and hung the navy blazer and pants in the closet. She unloaded her laptop onto the desk and took her toiletry bag across the hall. The bathroom was just as pretty as the guestroom. Seeing the tray of paper hand towels, decorated with little blue and yellow flowers, the new bar of soap still in its pretty wrapper, and the little folded triangle on the toilet paper roll, Charlie had to grin. How in the hell Martha had been able to room with her, she truly didn't know. Perhaps Martha's tidiness was an innate characteristic that enabled her to be so perfectly suited for her job as an accountant. Everything lined up in a row, the answer just waiting to be tabulated.

As for herself, her life had never been neat and tidy, and yet there was just something about having a jumbled mess, a puzzle to solve, that she found fascinating. Giving her hands a quick wash, she left the bathroom and went downstairs to truly begin her vacation.

"God, that was even better than I remembered," Charlie said as she sat back from the table.

"Thanks," Martha said, standing to begin clearing the dishes.

"Here, I'll do that. You cooked. I'll wash," Charlie offered.

"No, I'm just going to stick them in the dishwasher. How about you pour us another glass of wine?"

Charlie did so, and with the dishwasher humming, the two women took their wine into the living room. Settling in a large, overstuffed chair, Charlie took a sip of her wine. "You've done a great job, Martha. Everything is so pretty. You've really made a home for yourself."

"Okay, now that we've established I'm a Martha Stewart wannabe, and you are the reincarnation of Emily Post, enough with the polite chit-chat. How the hell are you really, and don't give me any of that 'I'm fine, never better' bullshit."

Taken aback, Charlie could only stare across the coffee table. "Wow, where did that come from?"

Martha tucked her legs up beneath her and shook her head. "Honestly? Have you looked in a mirror lately? Have you gone all earth-mother? They make products now that could easily conceal those circles under your eyes, and what's up with your hair?"

"Anything else?" Charlie asked, not sure if she'd been insulted or if Martha was the first person in ages to be brave enough to state the truth.

"You know I love you, right?"

That Charlie did know. Sighing, she sat back and nodded. "Yeah, even if you have a funny way of showing it. But, please, feel free to tell me what you really think."

"All right, I will," Martha said. "If you needed a loan, all you had to do was ask."

"What? Why on earth would you think that? I do have a paying job, you know."

Martha shrugged. "How could I not? I mean, have you seen what you're wearing? Charlie, the grunge look might be making a reappearance, but, honey, it is definitely not a good look on you."

When Charlie couldn't come up with a single thing to say about the torn jeans or the bulky, oversized sweater she was wearing, Martha continued, "Look, I wouldn't say anything except that I love you very much. And, Charlie, my job might not be as exciting as yours, but I do know how to add. What I'm seeing doesn't add up. And, at the risk of you telling me to shove it, don't tell me you are just peachy."

"Why the fuck does everyone suddenly seem to think I'm on the brink of falling into some abyss of depression?" Charlie asked. "I'm a fucking grown ass woman, and if I don't want to put on any fucking makeup, fix my fucking hair, or wear fucking clothes that don't have fucking men drooling all over me, then I don't see how in the fuck that is anybody's fucking business but my own!"

"I think that must be some kind of record."

"What?" Charlie wondered if the drive up from Texas had taken more out of her than she thought as she was having a tough time keeping up.

Martha took a sip of her wine and then set the glass on the table, lifting both of her hands, all ten fingers spread. "Let's see, 'why the fuck', 'what the fuck', 'fucking grown ass woman', 'fucking makeup', 'fucking hair'…" For each utterance of the f-word, Martha curled a finger into her palm. With the first hand now a fist, she shook her head and continued. "Then we have 'fucking clothes', 'fucking men drooling', 'how in the fuck', and, finally, 'nobody's fucking business'." With all but the pinky finger of her second hand counted, she looked across the space, giving her head a tilt.

"Oh, fuck you," Charlie said, defeated as Martha grinned and tucked her pinky finger in as well. "How on earth do you remember all that?"

"I'm very good with numbers and repetitive patterns," Martha said as she stood and came to where Charlie was sitting, kneeling at her side. "I'm also a very good listener, and, sister, if there has ever been somebody who needs an ear, it's you. I promise, I won't judge, I won't interrupt, I'll try not to tell you how to live your life, but I also promise, you're safe here with me. For God's sakes, Charlie, talk to me before you are so deep in the abyss you've fallen into that you can't find your way out."

"What if I'm already too deep?" Charlie asked.

"Then, honey, I'll just have to come in after you." Martha gave her a hug and then sat back on her heels. "And, we both know I won't give up until I'm satisfied all the columns align and we find the answer."

* * *

CHARLIE UPENDED the last of the second bottle of wine into her glass. Hours had past as she poured out all the emotions she'd kept bottled up inside. She wasn't sure if it was the wine that made her feel light headed, or if it was the weight that seemed to lift from her with every confession she made. She divulged that sometimes her job had her so scared that she didn't know if she could function. That she continued to take training, to push herself to the limit, so that no one would think she was weak. She admitted that sometimes all she wanted to do was cuddle up in bed and stay there for days. Leaving nothing out, she told Martha about the night of the sting and how she'd fallen apart in the bathroom, how she'd felt so filthy.

As Martha had promised, she didn't judge Charlie for the anger or the guilt. She didn't judge her for the countless nights Charlie had cried herself to sleep. When Charlie felt she couldn't go on, Martha would open her arms and hold her until she felt stronger. Her friend did exactly what Charlie needed... she just listened.

"I keep telling myself that, with time, things will get better, you know?"

"Honey, if you're waiting for some magic timer to buzz and make it all go away, I hate to say it, but you might as well wait for some leprechaun with a pot of gold to come riding in on a unicorn."

Charlie shook her head. "No more wine for you."

"I'm serious. Charlie, you used to have fun and now, hell, I had to beg you to come visit me. I know you're a good agent. I know you want to serve your country, but, honey, at what price? Hell, when was the last time you just did something for fun?"

"I took some training—"

"Oh my God! You just proved my point. You took some training? Seriously? That's all you've been doing for years. Face it, you're Bill Murray."

"I know you said I look like crap, but really? Gee, thanks."

Martha giggled and shook her head. "You know what I mean. Like in that movie, *Groundhog Day*. You keep waking up and repeating the same day over and over again." She reached over and tucked a curl behind Charlie's ear. "It is time to kick the furry little sucker into the abyss and climb out and move on."

"What happened to the 'don't tell me how to live my life' promise?" Charlie asked.

"I said I'd *try* not to, but we both know that isn't going to happen," Martha said, unapologetically. "And, evidently I'm not the only person to tell you this."

"No one has ever called me Bill Murray," Charlie countered, sipping her wine.

"I don't mean that. I mean you said everybody was trying to tell you what a sad ass life you're leading. Who did you mean?"

Charlie sighed. "First of all, I never said anything about leading a sad ass life. I am perfectly content with my life, thank you very much!"

"Sure you are," Martha said with a grin. "You forget, girlfriend, I've seen you very contented and this…" she paused to wave her hand up and down in front of Charlie's body, "this, is definitely not contentment."

"I think you're in the wrong field, Martha. You should have signed up to be an interrogator or something."

"No, I don't give a shit about what makes most people tick, but I do care about you. So, who was this guy?"

"How do you know it wasn't a woman?"

"I'm also good at statistics. And, since I'd have to kill you if I found out that you finally opened up to some other woman instead of calling your best friend, I decided to go with the other half of the options available. So, come on, please tell me it's someone you're seeing."

"No, not seeing," Charlie said. "Just a guy I worked with on this last assignment. His name is Dillon and he's with the FBI. One of the good guys." She turned her head and gave Martha a long look.

"He's called a couple of times just to check in. In fact, he sort of reminds me of you. You know, like a dog with a bone?"

Martha grinned. "So, he cares about you, huh?"

Charlie shook her head. "Like I said, we were partnered on and off for the past six months." She paused and smiled. "And before you get ready to play match-maker, I blew that chance when I refused to date him."

"What? Why would you do that? Do you know how hard it is to find a good guy?"

It was Charlie's turn to wave her hand in the air as if pushing away the question. "Job, temporary assignment, different career paths." Catching her friend rolling her eyes, she sighed. "Yeah, I know, but he's a good friend, and Dillon moves around as much as I do. Besides, he and his partner Lucy are a perfect team and in demand all over. They are a perfect match."

"So? It's not like he's married to her is he? Wait, he isn't, is he? This Dillon just lost his good guy status if you ask me," Martha said. "Why would he ask you out if he's with Lucy? That's a pretty shitty thing to do!"

Charlie shook her head. "I don't know. I mean, look at me. Why would he even think about asking Bill Murray out when Lucy is so beautiful? She has the silkiest hair, these incredibly soulful eyes, the sweetest smile, the patience of a saint, and the cutest little pointed ears. She's just perfect."

Martha's eyes narrowed. "So, she's what, a Vulcan?"

Charlie laughed. "No, she's a German Shepherd. Dillon trains agents in the K-9 unit when he's not out working cases himself."

"God, I'd forgotten what a smartass you are," Martha said, tossing a throw pillow at her. "But, back to the real point. You said he also talked to you? About what?"

Sighing, Charlie tucked her legs underneath her and hugged the pillow. "He told me that my life is pretty awful. That I work too hard, push myself too much, volunteer for any and all missions, yada yada yada."

"And?"

"Well, he didn't call me Bill Murray but he did seem to wonder if I'm really a girl—even though he saw me stark naked." She gave a strangled laugh. "Hell, maybe you're both right. Have I really forgotten what it's like to just be a woman?"

Charlie leaned her head back against the sofa as exhaustion washed through her. She couldn't remember not feeling tired. Was this how she wanted to feel for the rest of her life? Why bother getting out of bed if this was all she had to look forward to? Turning her head to look at Martha, she said, "If I admit that I need to reevaluate my life, will you let me go to bed?"

"No, but I'll let you get some sleep if you promise that moving on includes meeting new people and not just a change of locale. You're a young, healthy, beautiful, intelligent woman, Charlize Elena Fullerton. It is far too soon for you to say this is the best it's going to be."

"Make up your mind, Martha Louise Transom. First I'm a fashion plate for the grunge movement, then I'm Bill Murray, and now I'm gorgeous?"

Martha laughed. "I promise, you are all three, but, we're going to be working on retiring the first two."

"All right…"

"Starting tomorrow," Martha qualified. "And you have to pinky swear."

"Seriously? What are we, twelve?"

"No, as my best friend said, 'we are grown ass women who are going to make the most out of our lives'."

Charlie smiled. "You know, for an accountant, you sure do take a lot of liberties with adding a bunch of words I didn't say." When Martha just smiled, Charlie stuck out her hand, her pinky finger crooked. Martha hooked her pinkie and they shook. Martha then stood and pulled Charlie to her feet.

"I'd offer to help you clean up this mess, but I'd hate to tarnish your image, Ms. Stewart," Charlie said as she kicked aside an empty chip bag, and saw several other crumpled bags and open containers of things she couldn't honestly remember tasting. "God, did we really eat all that crap?"

"We did and don't worry about it. I'll clean up. You need to get some sleep. We've got a very busy day planned tomorrow."

"Planned? I don't remember planning anything," Charlie said, as they walked to the stairs.

"Don't you worry. Just consider me your personal vacation planner. I promise, you're going to love it."

Too tired to argue, Charlie just nodded. "Good night, Martha."

"Good night. Oh, and Charlie?"

Charlie turned back to look down the staircase. "Yes?"

"I really am glad you're here."

"I'm glad too." Charlie made it up another three steps before she turned around again. "Hey, what happened to blowing me away? All we did was talk about me." Martha's smile had Charlie's lips turning up. "Wow, that good, huh?"

"Unbelievable, but I think I'll save it. It can be the carrot I dangle in front of you while I kick your ass when you start to dig your heels in."

Charlie couldn't help but laugh. "I love you, you big goofball."

"I love you, too. Now, go to bed."

CHAPTER 4

"Seriously, Martha, I'm done." Charlie crossed her arms over her chest, refusing to give in.

"Ohhh, is that your big tough 'don't mess with a federal agent' look? Am I supposed to start cowering now and confessing to every unsolved crime?"

"I have been tweezed, plucked, trimmed, painted, waxed, poked, and prodded. I've been pounded, boiled, and dunked into an ice bath. I'm telling you, I am done, finished, through. So, exactly what part of finito don't you understand?"

Martha extended her little finger and wagged it up and down. "Pinky swear, so lose the attitude, put your arms down, and go try this on." Martha held out the hanger again, and when Charlie didn't immediately reach for it, Martha added, "Didn't your grandmother always tell you to make sure you have nice undies on?"

"I'm pretty damn sure she didn't mean those kind of undies," Charlie said.

"Aw, come on, Charlie." The hanger swung back and forth, like a pendulum. "See the pretty little panties? The sexy as shit bra? Come on, girlfriend. You know you can't wait to see how they look on." Martha tilted her head. "Unless, of course, it's been so long since you've actually worn something sexier than a sports bra and grannie panties that you can't remember there are actual hooks and lace involved? Wait, let me get my phone. I'm sure there must be some video on YouTube—"

"Give me those," Charlie snapped, reaching out and snatching the hanger from Martha's hand. Not because she wanted to try them on, but because she heard several customers giggling, obviously loving the ridiculous conversation. "I could so take you down," she muttered as she whirled around and stomped towards the dressing room. "I'm getting a little tired of the stick. Where's the damn carrot you promised?"

"Be a good girl and model for me, and I'll not only take you to Starbucks, I'll buy you a piece of carrot cake and we'll talk," Martha promised, leaning against the wall opposite the door that Charlie had practically slammed in her face. After a few muttered words, Charlie called out. "I don't see why I have to get new underwear. It's not like anyone is going to see it."

"That just makes me want to cry," Martha said. "Stop being a brat and show me."

A few moments later the door unlocked, and Charlie allowed Martha into the dressing room. "Wow! You've got boobs!"

"Very funny. You've seen my boobs, my butt, my everything today," Charlie retorted. "When you said spa day—"

"I meant every word," Martha said, cutting her off. Placing her hands on Charlie's shoulders, she turned her to face the full-length mirror. "You can't tell me that you don't look incredible."

Charlie looked at her reflection, her determination to remain pissed slipping away. When Martha removed her hands, Charlie turned and then stared back over her shoulder. "Okay, fine. They look pretty good."

"Pretty good? Girl, you look hotter than shit. How you can be so skinny and have such great tits and an ass I'd die for, I'll never know." She reached out and hugged her friend. "Seriously, Charlie, you look great. Now, wait here, I'll go get the rest."

"The rest? Oh no you did not!"

"Of course I did," Martha said, pulling open the door. "You can't just have one set of undies. What would your granny think? I'll be right back."

Charlie shook her head, but turned back to the mirror. Her hair had been washed, trimmed and styled into a very flattering bob. Her eyebrows plucked, she'd had both a manicure and a pedicure, all ten nails painted a deep ruby red. She'd gritted her teeth during the Brazilian wax and then sat naked in the steam room until she thought she'd melt right down the drain. She'd shrieked like a little girl when Martha pulled her into the cold pool. Every muscle had been pounded and massaged and every inch of her body moisturized. She'd handed over a small fortune to replenish her almost non-existent make-up supply. And now, staring at a woman she hadn't really seen in what seemed like forever, a smile curled her lips, and she had to admit, she didn't look half bad.

* * *

CHARLIE LIFTED her Venti size Caramel Macchiato with extra caramel and took a sip, then brought a forkful of the carrot cake to her mouth. "As good as this cake is, I was expecting something completely different. Today has been surprisingly okay, but again, it's been all about me. When are we going to get to the 'knocking my socks off' bit?"

"I'm glad you asked," Martha said, looking around the small café.

"And why do you keep checking to see if anyone is listening? Exactly what have you gotten yourself into? Please don't tell me I've gone through all this just so when I visit you in prison, you won't be embarrassed by how I look."

Martha laughed and shook her head. "All right. Here's the real carrot. We're going to get all gorgeous and then, my friend, I'm going to take you out on the town. Well, only part of the town, but believe me, you'll understand it's the only place to be. Charlie, it's absolutely amazing. It's the hottest club in D.C. and we'll dance and... hey, you're totally blowing that sexy look," Martha said from across the table. "Close your mouth; you look like a fish."

Charlie snapped her mouth shut, only to open it a second later. "I am not going out to some crowded as shit club and don't you even think about wagging that pinky finger. I did not agree to go dancing."

"Oh come on," Martha said. "Did you honestly think you were going to go through all this so you could... what? Sit at home and watch television?"

"What's wrong with that? I don't have a lot of time to just veg out. Some carrot that is."

Martha took the last bite of her slice of lemon pound cake and leaned forward. "That, my friend, is where you are so wrong. You'll be eating those words when you come out with me tonight. And, Charlie, I'll make you another deal. If it doesn't knock your socks off, I'll not only clean up after you, I'll wait on you hand and foot. You won't have to move your ass off that couch until your vacation is over."

"Hmmm, you'll wait on me? Do everything I ask? Rub my back—"

"I'll even rub your feet. Come on, Charlie, please just give it a try."

Charlie sat back and sighed. How could she say no to a woman who had been there every time she'd needed her since the day they'd met? "Okay, fine. You win. I'll go, but on one condition... the moment I decide I've had enough, we come home."

"But, not before you give it a real chance," Martha countered. "No running for the door the moment we get there. No pulling a Cinderella and going home the moment the clock strikes twelve.

Deal?" She held out her pinky and Charlie laughed even as she shook her head.

"I'm so not falling for that again, but yes, you've got a deal. I'm yours until at least one minute past midnight."

Martha smiled and drained her cup of Chai tea. "Great. Then one more stop and we can go home for a little nap before we get ready to go."

"What stop? I'm ready for a nap now," Charlie said, finding her coffee cup plucked from her hand the moment she took her last sip.

"You don't honestly think I'm going to let you out of the house in anything you brought do you? Not with what's in those pink bags. I'd offer to loan you something to wear, but I'm like a foot taller than you."

"And you're a math person?" Charlie said, slipping off the tall stool to stand next to her friend, looking up. "Six inches maybe."

"Whatever, shortie," Martha said, smirking as she patted Charlie on top of her head.

The boutique Martha took her to was the first shop Charlie had stepped into that hadn't been a super-store since she could remember. Looking at the tag hanging from the dress, she whistled. "Do you know how many pairs of jeans I could get at Wal-Mart for this amount?"

"Nope, and don't care. This would look great on you," Martha said, handing her another dress. "Go try those on and I'll bring you some shoes."

Knowing that to argue was futile, Charlie had the first dress on by the time Martha pushed back the curtain. "Well, what do you think?" Charlie asked.

"When was the last time you bought a dress?" Martha asked.

"I don't know. I don't have much of a need for dresses in my job. Why?"

"Because those boobs you had in that sexy bra are lost in that dress. It's got to be at least one..." she paused, checking the tag, "make that two sizes too big. Go on and try on the other and I'll get a smaller size. Oh, and here, you can try these on as well."

Before Charlie could speak, the curtain closed again as Martha disappeared, leaving two shoe boxes in her wake. Charlie slipped out of the dress and into the second one. It was a deep pumpkin color with metallic threads woven throughout that actually seemed to sparkle when she turned to look at her butt.

"That's much better," Martha said, causing Charlie to jump.

"God, sneak up on a girl why don't you?"

Martha ignored her. "Besides being a little too long, that looks great on you."

"Too long? Hell, I thought it was too short."

"You thought wrong." Hanging the dress she'd gone to get on a hook, Martha opened the first shoebox. "You're so lucky you don't wear a size ten. I have such a hard time finding shoes but these are gorgeous. They will look yummy with the pumpkin."

The shoes were brown suede, scalloped around the edges and while the heels were four inches, they weren't stilettos. Charlie slipped her feet into them and stood once more staring at her reflection. When she reached to tug down the hem, Martha slapped her hand away. "Cut it out. You look perfect. Okay, those are both keepers. Try on the black."

"I really don't need two dresses," Charlie said.

"Every girl needs a little black dress," Martha said, the dress off the hanger and already unzipped. "Stop complaining and admit you're having fun. Oh wait, take off your bra. We can't have bra straps showing."

Charlie was soon pulling the black dress over her head. The difference in sizes was instantly apparent. Narrow straps held up a bodice, that despite its plunging neckline, clung to her breasts, went over her shoulders, leaving her entire back bare. The skirt was full and flared when she gave a little twirl.

"Wow, Charlie, that's even better than the pumpkin!" Martha said, squatting to lift the top of the second box.

"No… no black," Charlie said, shuddering at the memory of the last time she'd worn black heels.

Martha looked up at her and then nodded. "You're right. We need a pop of color. Hang on."

By the time they climbed into the cab Martha had hailed, Charlie was the proud new owner of not only the pumpkin dress and heels, but a pair of red stilettos to go with the black dress. It took both women to carry all the purchases they'd made throughout the day. Sinking back against the seat, Charlie shook her head. "Keep this up and I'll be asking for that loan."

Martha smiled and arranged the bags. "Too late. You already confessed that you buy everything at Wal-Mart." Reaching over, she took Charlie's hand. "Thank you, Charlie. I know I've been a bit bossy…"

She shrugged when Charlie rolled her eyes and said, "a bit?"

"Fine, a lot bossy, but only because I love you."

"I know. I love you, too, but if you don't get me home and to bed, I'm not going anywhere tonight."

* * *

"WELL, LOOK WHO'S BACK," Martha said as Charlie came down the stairs. "Shit, I barely recognize you, Charlie. You look incredible. Are you ready to go?"

Charlie ran her hand down her dress. "If I'm not now, I never will be."

"Relax. There is an entire bunch of carrots just waiting for you to nibble on."

When the cab dropped them off, Charlie could only stare. The line of people wrapped around the corner. "Good grief, it's going to take hours to even get to the door!"

"I know, isn't it great?" Martha said. "And, it's like this every single night."

"Great? By the time we get inside, *if* we get inside, it will be past midnight. There has got to be someplace else we can go."

Martha took her hand. "Absolutely not. *Runway* is the hottest club in town. Come on."

Charlie could do nothing but follow as Martha pulled her towards the front of the line. She could feel the stares of the people waiting as they passed them by. About to warn Martha that there was most likely about to be a riot for cutting in line, she came to an abrupt stop when Martha stopped walking.

"You're looking lovely tonight, Marty. Good to see you again. Have a great evening."

Charlie was sure her jaw was dragging along the floor as Martha gave the guy at the door a little wave, an assurance of, "We're going to have a blast," and then pulled Charlie through the entrance.

"Whoa! Since when does an accountant have such power?" Charlie asked.

Martha smiled and released Charlie's hand. "Let's just say I'm a good customer. Well, what do you think?"

It took her question for Charlie to forget about the line and easy entrance as she looked around. The only thing the club had in common with others she'd visited was that there were people everywhere. Even the music sounded more vibrant, the acoustics so well designed that you could actually hear the lyrics of the song being played. She saw long walkways and looking up, realized the club was multi-level.

"I have to admit, it's incredible."

"I told you it would be. Let's grab a drink."

Martha didn't wait for her reply, just turned and walked towards the massive bar. Charlie smiled. The somewhat shy woman who had been her roommate was gone. Martha looked absolutely incredible in the red sheath dress she was wearing, the fabric clinging to her curves. Instead of being embarrassed by her height, slouching or attempting to stand on the sidelines, Martha was walking—no, make that sashaying—through the club, her red heels making her even taller than when attending the parties Charlie had dragged her to on campus.

Seeing the hundreds of bottles of liquor behind the neon-lit bar, Charlie was impressed. The labels were all top shelf brands. She ordered a vodka-cranberry and watched the bartender pour the Grey Goose over ice, adding the cranberry juice. When Charlie opened her purse, Martha shook her head.

"Nope, tonight's on me."

"You don't have to do that," Charlie protested. "I really do get a regular pay-check."

"I know, but tonight is special. Consider it your belated birthday present."

Charlie returned her wallet to her purse and closed it. "All right, thank you." Sipping her drink, she people-watched. Everyone was obviously having a good time. People were laughing, bodies were gyrating on the floor, and Charlie realized that, for the first time in a long time, she wasn't looking at strangers and profiling them. Instead, she was simply having fun. When Martha set her empty glass on the bar, plucked Charlie's from her hand, and dragged her towards the floor, instead of protesting, Charlie did as she'd promised. She forgot her worries and simply went with the flow.

They had danced to several songs, both women even dancing with different partners, before they took a break as a set ended.

"Did you lose an earring?" Charlie asked, noticing that Martha was staring at the ground. "You better find it fast because once the dancing starts, you'll lose a hand trying to grab it."

Martha shook her head and looked up. "No, I was checking to see if your socks… well, your shoes were knocked off."

Charlie rolled her eyes. "No, but I am having fun. Want another drink?"

"No, I want to go to stage two."

"Stage two? Is that upstairs?" Charlie asked, noticing several people above them, most sitting in areas designed for conversation or viewing the floor below. "Oh, there really are runways?"

"Yes, they hold fashion shows here as well as concerts. I've been to both and they are great. God, you should have been here when the Crushing Stones played, they were unbelievable. But, that's for another day. Come on." She grabbed Charlie's hand and pulled her deeper into the club.

"Oh good, I need to visit the little girl's room," Charlie said as the restrooms came into view. When she had finished and was washing her hands at the sink, Martha was waiting, and for the first time since Charlie had arrived in D.C., her friend looked a little leery. "What's wrong?"

"How serious were you really? I mean last night when you said you want to reevaluate your life?"

Charlie didn't know if she was more surprised at the question or the fact that the woman asking it seemed unsure if she should have even asked it. Taking the time to consider that fact, she realized that she was ready for changes in her life. Everything within her was telling her it was time. Smiling, she ran her hands down her hips. "Well, since I've gotten rid of my granny panties, I'd say I'm good to go. Why?"

Martha smiled. "Just making sure, and you are going to be so glad those panties are from Victoria's Secret and not Wallyworld." Grabbing her hand yet again, the two left the bathroom. After looking around, she continued. "Now for the real fun. What I'm about to show you, to share with you, is the real carrot."

Charlie was puzzled as she watched Martha walking towards a curtain at the end of the hallway. "Where are we going? This isn't the way back to the club."

"Just follow me," Martha said, giving her a grin. "Pretend we're following that yellow brick road."

Yellow brick road? Was she talking about the Wizard of Oz? Well, there is a curtain but that guy on that stool looks a lot more like some sort of guard than a wizard. All these thoughts ran through Charlie's mind at lightning speed. Before she could ask Martha what exactly she'd meant, the man stood.

"Hello, Marty," the man said, giving a smile that lightened the serious expression he had been wearing.

"Hi! This is my friend, Charlie, and I just told her she's about to step into Oz," Martha said.

The man looked Martha over, his grin telling his appreciation. "Well, you are wearing ruby slippers, so…" he pulled an edge of the curtain aside and gave a little bow, "welcome and may you find the answers to your heart's desires."

Martha grabbed Charlie's hand and pulled her behind the curtain. "All right, what's going on?" Charlie asked, looking over her shoulder to see that the curtain had already closed behind them. "Who was that guy?"

"Just think of him as the man at the door to the Emerald City," Martha said, not giving an answer that made any sense. Martha opened a door and pulled Charlie inside, quickly shutting the door behind them.

"Okay, forgot that second mojito, you've obviously had enough. What in the name of God is going on, Martha?"

"Where's your sense of adventure?" Martha asked.

"Seriously, a janitor's closet?"

Martha reached out and gave her a hug. "Just wait, I promise you're going to be—"

"Yeah, knocked out of my socks," Charlie said, shaking her head.

Charlie watched as her friend reached for a mop handle, giving it a pull. When a door opened, Charlie just stared at the purple glow that filtered into the closet. "Why do I feel like you got your stories mixed up. First Oz and now Narnia?"

Martha laughed and stepped through the door, turning to look back. "Forget Oz and Narnia. Think more falling through the looking glass. Come on."

Charlie followed and the two stood at the top of a flight of stairs. "Martha—"

Turning towards her, Martha took both of her hands. "From here on, call me Marty."

"Wait, that guy at the door and that man at the curtain. They called you Marty—"

"Exactly."

Charlie took a deep breath. "Honey, I love you, but you're not making any sense."

Martha laughed and when Charlie put her hands on her hips and opened her mouth, Martha said, "Okay, okay. I'm sorry, it's just that I'm so excited to share this with you. Remember that club where we took those courses? The one in Houston? The one we loved?"

Charlie nodded, the mere mention of the club and the memories of what she'd experienced within its walls bringing a heat to her insides and a skip of her heartbeat. Suddenly, the curtain, the guard, and even the closet were making a little sense but it couldn't possibly mean what she thought it might. Could it? "Martha, are you telling me that... that there is some—"

"Marty," Martha corrected. "Picture it about a thousand times better. Once we're inside, you can choose to participate or just watch other people play. No pressure at all. The membership is very exclusive, and I'm sure I don't have to tell you, absolutely confidential. Oh, and we need to give you a name. How about... Tex?"

Charlie's head was spinning with what Martha had just revealed, but that suggestion stopped the rotation. "Tex? For God's sakes, Martha... Marty, do I look like some big burly cowboy?"

Martha laughed. "No, but you do look so delicious that every cowboy, politician, rock star, and any other warm-blooded man is going to be drooling. Oh, but if Tony is here tonight, he's mine."

"Tony?"

"He's this Greek hotelier who spun me on Roulette Night. He's sort of a switch, but then again, I might... oh, never mind. That story can wait for another day, too. So, back to your name? What do you want to use?" Martha grinned. "How about Alice?"

"No," Charlie said, a name coming to her that had her heart skipping another beat. "Not Alice... Rose."

"Okay, Rose it is. Are you ready?"

"God no, but what the hell, lead on, but remember, if I decide to go... we go."

"After midnight," Martha corrected. "Just stay with me, Rose, and I promise, you won't regret it."

They walked down the flight of stairs, the purple light becoming brighter with each step. The stairs ended at another door. When they passed through the door, there was a small room where a man stood behind a desk in the center of the space, looking up as they approached.

"Nice to see you again, Marty."

"Hi, Danny. I'd like you to meet my friend, Rose. Rose, this is Danny. He works security."

"It's nice to meet you, Rose. Have you got a guest pass?" Danny asked.

"Um, no—"

"She's my guest tonight," Martha said.

"Great. Once you've signed in and have a pass, don't forget to remove any electrical devices and put them in your locker."

"Will do," Martha said, gesturing for Charlie to follow her to a frosted glass window in the middle of the right wall. While they waited for it to slide open, Marty explained. "Submissives who participated on Roulette night received a month's membership and then Tony, well, Mr. Stravos, gave me a gift of an additional month's membership. Tonight, I'm paying it forward."

Before Charlie had a chance to ask about what she'd meant by Roulette, the window opened and a woman said, "Good evening, Marty."

"Hi. This is my friend, Charlize, and she's my guest tonight," Martha said, handing over her credit card.

"What happened to Rose?" Charlie whispered.

"They need your real name when you sign in," Martha explained and when Charlie pulled out her driver's license and handed it to the woman, she was surprised to have it returned with a sheaf of papers.

As she glanced at the top sheet, she looked up at Martha. "A non-disclosure agreement?"

"Yes, remember I said the membership is very confidential? Well, I meant it. This club has very high standards of confidentiality."

"I can understand that," Charlie said, reading through the document. In fact, despite Martha's dramatics, she was pretty impressed with the entire operation. Choosing a fake name was one thing, but that was only good if no one actually recognized you. While it was highly unlikely that anyone would know her, she knew that D.C. was the home of a great many recognizable public figures. This wasn't like the club above them. Granted, Runway was a fantastic club, but being seen dancing, watching a fashion show or a concert was pretty innocent. But if this subterranean club was anything like she was beginning to suspect, members would definitely not appreciate seeing their names splashed all over the news. However, with the guard at the curtain, the janitor's closet, Danny at the desk checking to make sure no recording devices were allowed inside, and now being required to sign a legally binding agreement not to disclose anything that might cause problems for any guests, she found she appreciated the owner's efforts to give more than lip service about security and discretion for those people who entered their club.

Charlie signed the NDA and passed it back to the attendant who thanked her and wished her a great evening before sliding the window closed again. "Great, we're good to go," Martha said, moving towards the lockers. "All right, as Danny said, no purses and nothing electronic are allowed inside. No cell phones, cameras, etcetera." As she was speaking, Danny pressed something that opened a locker. "We can share," Martha said, slipping her purse inside before turning back to Charlie.

When Charlie hesitated to hand over the small purse she'd borrowed from Marty for the evening, Marty tilted her head. "What's the matter? I promise our stuff will be absolutely safe."

Charlie shook her head and gave a self-deprecating grin. "It's not that," she admitted. "I just can't remember the last time I've not had my phone close. It's like an extension of my hand. I feel a little naked without it."

"Not tonight it's not," Martha said, plucking the bag from Charlie's hand and putting it away. "You're on vacation. Oh, your watch too." After Charlie handed it over, Martha shut the locker and grinned. "And, Rose, hopefully you'll be a lot naked by the time the night is over." Charlie rolled her eyes but felt a twinge of excitement run through her body.

Once everything was stowed away, Danny smiled. "Welcome to Black Light, Rose. You ladies have a good time."

"Oh, we will," Martha said, opening the door past Danny.

Charlie just stared once she was in the club. Forget Oz. Forget Narnia. Hell, forget the looking glass. Black Light was more than all three combined. While she wasn't a total novice or stranger to such clubs, never before had she felt... well, awed. There was an almost electric pulse in the air that was causing the small hairs on her arms to lift and her heart rate to speed up. She didn't know where to look first, and discovered it didn't matter. Everywhere she looked, she saw people in all states of dress and involved in scenes straight out of a BDSM lover's bucket list.

A woman, totally nude except for a collar around her neck, was kneeling before a man, his cock slipping in and out of her mouth. She would give a little yelp each time he'd slap the leash attached to the collar against her ass. From what Charlie could tell, if the pink stripes all across the woman's ass were any indication, she'd been on her knees for a long time. And that was within two feet of the door they'd entered. The smack of implements against flesh was causing her blood to heat, and the soft cries of women writhing in pleasure had her pulse fluttering.

"Oh my God, is that Jaxson Davidson?" Charlie asked, staring at a drop-dead gorgeous man whose face and body graced hundreds of magazines. "Shit, it is! And that's Chase Cartwright!"

"Yes, and the woman with them is Emma—the third person of their trio. She is a very lucky lady, but so incredibly nice that you can't be jealous... well, not for too long. They are not only a three-some, they own both Runway and Black Light. Want to meet them? Cha... I mean Rose? Rose?"

Charlie felt a nudge and looked over to see Martha grinning from ear to ear. "So, how are those carrots tasting?"

"Pretty delicious."

Martha laughed again. "Come on. We can grab a drink and I'll introduce you around. I don't see Tony, so it looks like I'll need to find another Dom tonight." Martha had taken one step before Charlie's hand stopped her.

"My God, she looks like a piece of art," Charlie said, nodding across the room. A crowd had gathered in front of a raised platform, but they didn't obstruct the view because the woman was suspended in the air.

"Ah, you're lucky. It's not often you can observe rope play. Not too many Doms are allowed to perform it. Jaxson and Chase enforce very strict safety rules. Come on, let's get closer. See that man in the black leather on the platform?" When Charlie nodded, Martha continued. "That's Owen. He must be giving a demonstra-tion. He's not only a dungeon master, he is a master of shibari."

As they walked across the room, Charlie was barely conscious of the other scenes she knew were occurring around her, but was very aware that her new panties were dampening. The suspended woman was gorgeous. She hung in the air, her body supported by nothing more than ropes. Intricate knots formed patterns along her arms and legs. Her breasts had been wrapped, both binding and enhancing their roundness. Pink nipples were taut, pointing towards the ceiling, and once they were within a few feet, Charlie could see more evidence of the woman's arousal. Her legs were spread wide, her glistening sex displayed. Her arms were bound together behind her back, long blonde hair cascading towards the floor.

Charlie watched as a man stepped forward, his hands reaching for the woman's breasts. As her nipples were plucked, the moan the woman gave caused Charlie to shudder. A second man moved between the woman's spread legs, his hands stroking along her thighs.

"Are you ready?" the man at her head asked.

"Yes… oh, yes, please, Master."

It was like a choreographed dance, the two men entering the woman at the same time. One pushing his cock into her mouth, the other her pussy, moving in perfect synchronization as they thrust. Charlie's breath caught in her throat as the men began to move faster. Not a single sound was made by the crowd of onlookers as they watched what was probably the most erotic scene she'd ever witnessed. Time seemed to slow as the men took their pleasure, cocks buried and hands constantly moving to caress the bound woman. Charlie felt her pulse pounding as with a roar, both men pushed deep, filling their partner with their release, again in perfect unison. When they pulled from her, one bent to kiss, suckle, and give her breasts little nips, the other to lick along her pussy, his tongue broadening to lap up her essence. Within moments, the woman's body, even bound by the ropes, jerked as she screamed and exploded with her climax.

"That was… incredible," Charlie whispered, as the crowd erupted into applause.

"Another reason why I love this club. They are always doing sexy demonstrations," Martha said.

Charlie was barely listening as she watched Owen take one

side and another man, his back to her, working with him to begin undoing the knots. She smiled to see that the woman's partners, stayed at her side, their hands never ceasing to stroke her body. It took several minutes before the woman was lowered to the floor, the remaining ropes removed. One of her partners lifted her into his arms, the other tucking a blanket around her as the trio walked away.

"Lucky lady," Martha said. "Aftercare with those two has got to be almost as good as the whole scene. Come on, let me introduce you to Owen."

Charlie turned her attention from the trio to see a man bending to pick up a piece of the discarded rope. Just seeing it in his hand, imagining it wrapped around her hands, her legs, her breasts, had Charlie's nipples tightening inside her new bra and her belly filling with butterflies.

But when the man straightened and turned, and his eyes met hers, Charlie's gasp was louder than the woman's moans had been. Forget her socks, she felt as if her entire world had been knocked out of alignment.

CHAPTER 5

The moment he looked up and met her eyes, his entire world tilted. It was Charlie, though a Charlie he hadn't yet met. He'd thought she was attractive from the moment they'd met, and yet, the woman standing before him, green eyes as wide as saucers, her mouth slightly open, was the most stunning woman he'd ever laid eyes on. He didn't hesitate, every instinct telling him that she was no more than a heartbeat from fleeing. Everything and everyone around him disappeared as he jumped from the platform and strode towards her. He was within a few feet when he saw her snap back into awareness and heard her speak.

"Oh my God! It's… it's Dillon!"

"What? Where?"

"Go! Go!" Charlie's voice sounded panicked.

"Rose, wait!"

Damn, he was almost there. If he had any doubts, the moment he heard the brunette call out the name, he knew Charlie belonged to him.

Charlie didn't wait. Dillon watched as she twirled around and began to run, blindly pushing through people. Dillon cursed, dodging around a couple, almost losing her in the crowd, but having a damned good idea of her destination. Changing direction, he maneuvered along the wall, catching sight of her as she cleared the crowd and made for the door. Increasing his pace, Dillon managed to get his arms around her waist, and well aware of her self-defense skills, pinned her against the wall, pulled her arms above her head and leaned his weight against hers, effectively caging her in.

"Hello, Rose," he said, her squirming doing nothing but causing his cock to stiffen.

"Let me go!" she hissed, attempting to lift her knee towards his crotch. He pressed in closer, feeling her tense when she became aware of his erection against her stomach.

"Not a chance in hell that's going to happen," he said. He might not understand how Charlie had turned up in D.C., on this night, in this club, but he had absolutely no intention of letting her get away.

"Please, Dillon... I- I can't-can't think... please, God, just let me go."

Dillon shook his head. "Remember how I told you I kicked myself for not following my gut that night?" He felt her still as he bent his head down, to speak a fraction of an inch from her lips. "I'm not a man to make the same mistake twice." With that, he crushed his mouth against hers. It only took a moment before she responded, her lips parting to allow him entrance. His tongue swept over hers, tasting, claiming, demanding as he deepened the kiss. He swallowed her moan, his cock protesting its confinement, her breasts smashed against his chest, her fingers moving to curl around the hands holding them in place. He didn't break the kiss until he needed a breath, and even then, only pulled away far enough to take in air. It was a kiss that had his heart pounding and the fact that Charlie was panting, the tip of her tongue tracing her bottom lip as if to soothe, told him that she'd not been unaffected. Smiling with the incredible pleasure he was experiencing, he was about to kiss her again, but he saw tears shimmering in her eyes before she dropped her head and his impression instantly shifted.

"Hey, look at me," he said, only to see her shake her head, but she was no longer attempting to get away. In fact, she buried her face against his chest, pushing closer. "Look at me," he repeated and when she didn't obey, he dropped one hand to place two fingers under her chin, tilting her face up. "Talk to me, Charlie," he said softly.

"You saw me," she said. "You saw me in a—a sex club. You- you think I'm—I'm a freak!"

He couldn't stop his bark of laughter. "Seriously? Where exactly do you think I'm standing?"

"Wha- what?"

Shaking his head, he bent to press his lips against hers in a gentle kiss. "Baby, I'm standing in the same club, and I sure as hell don't think you're a freak."

"You- you don't?"

For a woman he knew was incredibly fit, one who was physically able to defend herself against men twice her size, a woman so remarkably able to handle the stress of her profession, Dillon was surprised to hear the disbelief in her softly spoken question. Instead of speaking, Dillon bent to kiss her again, this time paying close attention to her reaction. Soft lips trembling beneath his own testified to her uncertainty but when her arms dropped to wrap around his neck, he felt her press her lips against his, giving him hope that he'd be able to assure her that he considered her to not only be an incredible woman, but one who stirred every cell in his body.

His hands didn't remain idle; he pulled her from the wall just enough to lift her, filling his palms with the globes of her ass, yanking her closer as her legs wrapped around his waist. She mewed into his mouth as he ground his cock against her. When he finally pulled back, he said, "Does that give you the answer?

You are the most amazing woman I've ever known." He kissed her again, this time her tongue dueled with his, her fingers woven in his hair. When they broke again, they were both panting. While he was ready to simply rip her panties off and push himself into her, he couldn't. This was a woman he'd come to not only desire, but to admire. Tightening his hold, he carried her to the bar, setting her down on a stool before taking her arms from around his neck and squeezing her hands. Hyperaware of her every reaction, he saw the uncertainty attempting to creep back into her eyes.

"Don't," he said softly. "I have every intention of showing you that I meant every word when I said I was your number one fan." He again used his fingers to lift her chin, his eyes locked to hers. It was time to get a bit of information. "This isn't your first time in a BDSM club is it?"

"Um, no…" she said, her face flushing so adorably. "Not my first, and I don't want to disappoint you, but, well, to be honest, I've not played much. I basically went to take a few classes in learning protocol and how to be a…"

"Submissive?" he offered when she didn't continue. Her blush deepened as she nodded, and he couldn't resist bending forward and giving her a quick kiss. "You are so gorgeous when you blush."

She gave him a quick smile and then offered a bit more information. "With graduation from college and then accepting a position with the DEA and all that involved, well, it's been a while… a long while."

"I'm glad." His instant response surprised him but was the absolute truth. Charlie was a grown woman who could certainly do whatever she wished, but when he thought about the astronomical odds of them being here, at Black Light, without any prior plans or even the barest discussion of their proclivities for a bit of kink, it again felt like fate had brought them together. "I'll be honored to reintroduce you to all sorts of possibilities." He loved the quick flare of desire that made her eyes sparkle. "Did you learn anything about hard limits?" he asked.

"A little," she admitted. "Those are things that you... I mean, I don't like?"

"Sort of but that's not a complete definition," Dillon corrected. "Unless you've experienced everything, then you really won't know what you like. A hard limit refers to something that you either have tried and don't wish to again, or it can be something that you have absolutely no desire to even try." He took the definition one step further. "And, your hard limits don't have to be chiseled in concrete. You might not want to try something now, but as you continue on your journey, you might decide to give a new experience a try."

"Isn't that a Dom's job? I mean, deciding what a submissive can take?" Charlie asked.

"A Dom's responsibility is to assure he meets his submissive's needs." He leaned against the bar but kept her hands in his. From what he'd learned so far and from her responses... both verbally and physically, he felt the need to move their discussion in a direction he hoped she'd agree it needed to take... a personal journey between them. "If we are talking about me, as a specific Dom, then I will tell you that while I will encourage you to try something, and will push you to your limits at times, but I will definitely never overstep the boundaries and ignore your hard limit list." He knew that it was a lot of information to take in at once and they could delve into a deeper conversation later. For now, he only needed to know what she had placed on her list... if she even had one. "How about we just concentrate on right now? What are you absolutely not wanting to experience tonight?"

She took a moment and then gave her answer. "I don't like blood in any form, I'm not interested in water sports either."

Dillon was surprised at the very short list. "That's not much of a list. Anything else?"

Her eyes dropped for a moment and he could see her body tense. "Wooden paddles... I don't like them anymore."

Remembering that had been the implement Sorenson had

used, and having seen the results of his sadistic use of what could have given Charlie pleasure as well as pain, Dillon could understand this limit.

"I promise, no paddles. Anything else?"

"I- I don't know... I've not tried everything."

"That's fine. Remember, lists can evolve and change with experience. Now, in your lessons, did you learn about safewords?"

This time there was no hesitancy in her response. "Yes, that's one of the first things we were taught." She paused and shook her head. "Though, since then, I've learned that it isn't the actual use of the word that matters... it's worthless when the man hearing it ignores it."

Dillon drew her closer. "That's true but I hope to God you realize that Sorenson isn't a Dom, honey. He's a..."

"Shithead," Charlie offered.

"That's one word," Dillon agreed. "I assure you that you won't have to worry about that with me, all right? You give a safeword and all action immediately stops." At her nod, he continued, "Black Light uses the standard safe words. Green for good. Yellow to pause the action, and Red to stop. Or, if you'd rather, you can choose your own."

"No, those are fine."

Dillon kissed her forehead and pulled back in order to be able to watch her eyes... they were so expressive, so telling. "I want you, Charlie. I want to have you writhing in pleasure and begging for more. But I need you to tell me, are you going to be all right exploring that pleasure here, in view of others, or would you prefer to play alone... without witnesses?" When she didn't answer, he leaned his forehead against hers. "I know what you went through with Sorenson and there is no wrong answer. You have absolutely nothing to prove."

She closed her eyes but only for a moment. When she opened them, he saw a difference in their depths. A desire, a need that he understood with her next words. "Yes, I do. Maybe not to you, but to myself. I need to replace that memory, and, Dillon, the only person I trust to do that with is you. And the only place is here."

He nodded, once again acknowledging the inner strength of this woman. "I promise you will have that new memory. Will you accept me as your Dom tonight, Charlie?"

Charlie had kept her eyes on his and nodded. "Yes, Dillon, I will.

"Thank you," Dillon said, feeling that he was not only accepting the responsibility of helping her make a new memory, but felt incredibly honored to be offered the gift of her submission.

"Now, is there anything you'd like to try tonight?" She seemed surprised he asked. "Charlie, I want us both to enjoy this."

She hesitated and then admitted "I'd like to try ropes," she said softly.

He felt a surge of pleasure at her answer. "You're a fan of shibari?"

"Yes... I mean no... I don't know. I've never experienced it. But, it was amazing to see that woman. The ropes, the knots were so... so intricate. It's like watching an artist create a masterpiece only with a body as his canvas and ropes as his medium." She flushed and shook her head. "I'm sorry, that sounds..."

"Perfect," he said, "that's exactly how I view it. So you enjoyed the demo?"

"Very much."

"I would love introducing you to rope play, but it took over two hours to set up that scene with Angelica and her Doms. How about we save that for another time?" Even though she nodded, he saw the flash of disappointment on her face. "However, that doesn't mean we can't start with a little taste." He could feel her pulse jump with his fingers moving to trace her throat.

"Ready?"

She nodded again and when he lifted her off the stool, she wrapped herself around him but then said, "Wait!"

"Babe, I've waited long enough." He slipped one hand under her dress, loving the gasp she gave as he palmed her sex. "You look absolutely beautiful in this dress. The color reminds me of my favorite pie... pumpkin." He gave her a quick kiss. "And while I love the taste of your lips, it's time to taste the rest of you."

Her cheeks flushed as she said, "My- my shoe."

"What?"

She giggled and pointed back to where they'd been standing. He turned to see a lone brown heel propped against a leg of the stool. "Marty was right. She said this club would knock my socks off."

He grinned and set her down before squatting to pick up her shoe. Seeing her tilting a bit to one side, he slipped the shoe onto her foot. "That takes care of the shoe, now let's take care of the rest," Dillon said, kissing her lightly again before stepping back. With her permission and acceptance, he went into full Dom mode. "All right. From here on out, you'll call me Sir, understood?"

"Yes."

He didn't speak, didn't move his eyes from hers. She seemed puzzled, then flushed. "Oh, you mean starting now?"

"Yes, starting now," he said with a grin.

"Oh, okay, I- I mean, yes, Sir."

"Infractions of the rules will earn penalties. Understood?"

"Yes, Sir."

"Good girl," he said, taking her hand and looking around the club at the areas available for play. Spying one that would work for what he had planned, he gave her hand a squeeze, looking down at her. "Ready to play?"

"Yes, Sir."

They moved across the room and he wasn't the least bit surprised to see the brunette watching them. He was pleased to know that Charlie had someone watching her back but not interfering unless needed. He was even more pleased when Charlie gave the woman a small wave as if to assure her that all was well. The brunette smiled, waved back and only then moved away. Once they reached the vacant station, Dillon pulled Charlie close, bending to kiss her again. He didn't want her tense or anxious. He wanted her soft and compliant. He cupped her breasts, his thumbs strumming over nipples that were so hard they were easy to find despite the fact that they were covered by her clothing. He continued to plunder her mouth until she was mewling, pushing her breasts into his hands. Stepping away, he said, "Don't move."

"Ye... yes, Sir," she whispered before he saw her tongue come out to travel over her bottom lip. It was so sweet, so innocent, and yet, God, it caused his cock to jerk again as he imagined her tongue on his flesh. He left her to move just a few feet to the cabinet he and Owen had opened earlier. Taking a few lengths of rope, he returned to her. He watched her eyes drop to his hands where he was running the white hemp through his fingers.

"Do you know what shibari means?"

"Um, binding with rope... Sir?"

"No, but most people believe that to be true. Actually, Kinbaku is the correct word. It is Japanese, meaning the art of binding, using rope. Kinbaku-ki, is the word used to describe the bondage art. But the word shibari actually reflects what you said earlier. Shibari translates to mean intricately tie." He draped the ropes around his neck, loving the fact that her eyes lifted to watch every move. Stepping forward, he said, "Turn around." Once she had, he slowly unzipped her dress, placing kisses along her spine as the dress parted. He slid the fabric from her shoulders, kissing each one and causing her to give those delightful little mews each time he gave her skin a little nip, his tongue quickly soothing the slight pain. He allowed the dress to slip to the floor where it pooled at her feet.

"Beautiful," he said softly. His heart skipped a beat as he looked at her, so perfect, so trusting. He'd played before but never once had felt this way. Leaving Texas had been hard... not because he didn't want to return to his own home, but because he'd left without knowing more about this woman. And now? Charlie's very presence, her appearing from nowhere, had his blood racing through his veins, his breath catching in his throat. He could stare at her all day and yet couldn't resist the absolute need to touch her again. Still standing behind her, but moving closer to wrap his arms around her, pressing his body into hers. His thumbs again found her nipples, which were attempting to poke through the fabric of her bra. When she leaned her head back against him, her eyes closing, he bent to kiss her cheek. With a flick, he released the front closure of her bra, the cups parting, allowing her breasts to spill into his hands. They were perfect, round and soft, each pillow topped by a puckered nipple that reminded him of ripe raspberries. He traced her areolas, looking over her shoulder, watching as her flesh pebbled into goose bumps. When he lifted his fingers, she moaned, arching up as if to find his hands again.

Long lashes laid against her skin, fluttering slightly. "Open your eyes," he said, waiting until her eyelids fluttered and opened. Little flecks of gold seemed to float in the emerald depths. "Now your mouth," he ordered. She hesitated but obeyed, her lips parting. "Good girl," he said, bringing his index fingers to her mouth. Giving his next order to suck, he slid his fingers into her mouth. The feel of her tongue swirling around his flesh, the sight of her cheeks hollowing in and out as she suckled, had his cock demanding it take his fingers' place. "Release," he said, and when she did, he returned his fingers to her breasts, this time placing his wet fingertips directly on her nipples.

She gasped, and arched again, her saliva transferred to her skin combined with his touch causing her nipples to tighten further. His thumbs joined his fingers, plucking and pinching until she was trembling. Releasing her only long enough to turn her to face him, he bent to take a nipple into his mouth, his tongue adding moisture as it flicked and played over the taut bud. He suckled hard until she moaned, her hands coming up to grip his shoulders.

After giving her second breast the same attention, he straightened and removed her bra completely.

"Beautiful," he repeated as she stood in nothing but her panties, her stockings, and her shoes. He realized that her eyes had darted from his, returning but not meeting his gaze. A glance told him that a small group had gathered. Speaking softly, he asked, "Color?"

"Gr- green... yellow-green, Sir."

"Do you want a blindfold?" He wasn't going to give her the option of changing her mind about their location, but he had no problem offering her a chance to not have to see anyone witnessing their play.

"No... no, Sir."

"Just keep your eyes on me, Charlie. No one else exists but the two of us." She nodded, her eyes meeting his. "Good girl. Put your arms out, palms together." When her arms extended, he pulled the first rope from around his neck. "Splay your fingers." Once she had, he began, not starting with either end, instead, found the center of the rope and began to weave the ends between her fingers. He went slowly, pleased when her attention remained on what he was doing, watching each movement of the rope ends as they wove in and around each other. He continued wrapping the ropes around her wrists, adding intricate knots every few turns of the ropes.

"They look like flower buds," she said softly, a smile on her lips.

"White rosebuds for my little yellow Rose," he said, bending to kiss a rope flower before continuing. "This is a basic corset pattern." He continued to work and then said, "Do you own a corset?"

"No, Sir."

"We'll correct that soon," he said, loving the flush that stained her cheeks and the quick flick of her eyes to his before dropping back to where his hands continued to bind her. At her elbows, he added a knot at each bend when he added another length of rope. "Shibari isn't meant to take away your freedom. When we do a full session, you'll discover that being bound so completely, will give you an incredible sense of peace, the liberty just to be. For now, let it assure you that we are bound by the very art. Lift your arms."

She obeyed and he used the next length of rope to secure her arms to a chain that descended from the ceiling. "Color?" he asked.

"Green, Sir," she answered instantly.

With her arms secure, he ran his hands down her sides, his thumbs stroking her flesh as he bent to kiss her, loving the fact that she arched into him and loving it even more when he felt her shudder as he hooked his fingers into the waistband of the white lace panties. He slowly peeled them down, her arousal evident by the soaked gusset and her scent filling his nostrils. She was bare, but he still needed to see more. "Step out." When she did, he moved the pile of clothing to one side and then said. "Spread your legs."

The next rope was used to form a ladder pattern from her knee to her ankle before being secured to a ring in the floor. Once both legs were secure, he knew the crowd most likely expected him to choose an implement to use. He had other plans and could no longer deny the need to taste her. Kneeling before her, he cupped her ass in his hands and brought her to his mouth. She shuddered with the first flick of his tongue though it was the lightest of touches. He continued to lick, to tease, never going near her clit which was already out of its hood, trembling with need. She was soaking wet, every drop taken into his mouth tasting of the finest ambrosia as he used every lick, every taste, every mew and shudder to imprint this woman on his heart. It didn't take long before her small mews turned to pleas.

"Please... oh, please... may I come... please, Dillon!"

Her soft request, the absolute need in her voice, had his heart skipping again. She hadn't addressed him as "Sir" and yet that didn't matter. The only thing he cared about was the desire to pleasure her, to drive her insane with need, to erase Sorenson and the memories of that night, to replace them with memories she'd treasure.

"Yes, come as often and whenever you want," he granted, finally grazing her clit with his teeth before sucking it into his mouth and giving it a small bite. She tasted better than he'd even dreamed she would in the months he'd admired her in Texas.

"Oh, God!" she shouted, her body jerking as she came. He continued to flick his tongue across the bundle of nerves, alternating with suckling. Removing his hands from her ass, he spread the petals of her vulva open, exposing the soft, pink inner lips of her cunt. Sliding his tongue inside, a fraction of an inch at a time, she was soon begging.

"More... oh, please... more..."

"Such a greedy girl," he teased, removing his mouth and loving her whine of loss and then her gasp of pleasure as he replaced his tongue with two fingers. "So tight. God, I can't wait to feel your cunt hugging my cock."

"Yes!" she shouted.

He grinned, enjoying every moment watching one of the most in control people he'd ever met coming apart. "Yes, what?"

"Please, Dillon... please fuck me!"

He didn't have to be asked twice. Removing his fingers, he bent forward and took a last, long, slow lick before standing. She was shuddering, her nipples as hard as diamonds, her eyes locked on his hands as he unfastened his pants and allowed his erection to spring free. Grabbing a condom from a bowl, he ripped it open and rolled it over his cock.

"Oh my God," she groaned. "You'll... you'll never fit."

"Believe me, I will fit just fine," Dillon countered, quickly releasing the knots that kept her feet bound to the rings. Moving in front of her, he lifted her, positioning his cock at her entrance. "Every single inch will be buried in your sweet heat." She moaned as he began to impale her, and though he wanted to bury himself balls deep in one thrust, he knew she needed the time to stretch, to relax, to accept his girth.

"God, you make the sweetest sounds," he said, pushing in another inch, and then another. She moaned, shook her head, and yet she never asked him to slow. Her flesh clenched around him, and yet her copious amounts of cream eased his entrance. Finally, when his balls were nestled against her pussy, he bent forward. "Let go. The only one biting that lip is me." She released her lip and he took her mouth as he began to move. She was so incredibly tight and so amazingly responsive. Her nipples rubbing against his t-shirt had him wishing he'd taken the time to remove it, wanting to feel her breasts against his chest. Her legs wrapped around his waist and her soft moans and cries were music to his ears. It was far too soon when he felt his balls tightening.

"Come for me," he demanded as he lifted his mouth from hers. "Come with me!" He tilted her slightly, going deeper, the slap of his hips against her body adding notes to their song until, with a cry, she sang her pleasure and he roared his as they found their release at the same instant.

He held her close, kissing her softly, nipping her lip, her neck, and giving his own groan as she added her mark to his skin, biting his shoulder. He welcomed the pain of the bite as it proved his Charlie was really there, and this wasn't just a wishful dream. When she'd given the last shudder, he slowly withdrew and carefully disengaged her legs, allowing her to stand again. It took only a moment to discard the condom and tuck himself back inside his pants.

Putting an arm around her waist, he reached up and unhooked the rope, bringing her arms down. She gave a soft groan and he lifted her into his arms, then bent to scoop up her clothes from the floor. The soft applause of the people who observed their play followed them as he carried Charlie to a seating area nearby. He took a large leather chair and cradled her on his lap.

"Water, Sir?" a server offered.

"Thanks," Dillon said, accepting two bottles of water from one of the staff. Uncapping the first, he said, "Sit up, baby, drink this."

"I'm good," she said, snuggling closer.

Dillon chuckled. "No, you're great, but I still want you to sit up and drink this." He adjusted her until she sighed and reached for the bottle, giving a giggle when they both realized her hands were still bound.

"Here," he said, placing the bottle at her lips. She took several swallows before pulling back. Dillon drank the rest and then began to undo the knots, releasing her hands. "So, still a fan of rope play?" he asked.

"Yes, definitely," she said as he set the ropes aside and began to massage her arms. "I thought my arms would be strained, but they weren't at all."

"That's because I didn't lift you off the floor. Even with full suspension, like you witnessed earlier, when done correctly, will never cause your muscles to strain. The ropes support your weight. Shibari requires an entirely different set of knots and combination of ropes."

"That's why it takes so long?"

"It can. The more intricate the pattern, the more of the body being bound, determines the time. You'll see when we do a full session."

"Hmmm, that's something to look forward to," she said, wrapping her hands around his neck and bending to kiss him. Dillon held her close for several minutes, loving the feel of her in his arms, her little wiggles causing his cock to stir again. Setting her up, he removed the ropes from her legs and then moved her to her feet. "Let's get you dressed."

"Oh... God, I- I forgot," she said, and he loved the fact that she sounded surprised and yet not truly embarrassed. He remembered the sting; that night she'd also forgotten her nudity. Charlie was definitely a woman comfortable with her body. Picking up her dress, he grinned. "You realize that for the rest of my life, every time I see this color, I'm going to think of you?" He watched her look from the dress to him, her eyes widening when he slid a hand between her legs and then was shocked when she gave a little giggle.

"So every time you see me you're going to be craving pumpkin pie?" she asked.

His cock jerked and he shook his head. "No, I'm gong to be craving you." As if to prove his point, he removed his hand from her sex and took his sweet time giving each of his fingers a long slow swipe of his tongue. "Yum." Her face colored immediately as he began to slide the dress over her head.

"Dillon, the bra goes first."

"Not tonight it doesn't. The less you wear, the faster I'll get you naked and beneath me." He tucked her bra and panties into his pockets and then gathered the ropes and both bottles they'd emptied between them. Putting the bottles into a bin, he took her hand and dropped the ropes on the floor next to the cabinet.

"Why did you leave them on the floor?" she asked, when he didn't add them to the coils on several shelves.

"Every rope used will be washed and checked for any fraying," he said. "Safety first is important in any play, but when trusting a rope to support someone, safety becomes even more important."

He kept his arm around her waist as he scanned the room. Spotting Owen and the brunette who'd been standing with Charlie, he said, "I'm assuming that's Martha?"

"Oh, yes, but she goes by Marty here." Dillon nodded and guided her through the crowd towards the couple. As they got closer, Charlie said, "Wow, you look just like Owen. Are you twins?"

"No, Dillon is just lucky to look like his older brother," Owen answered before Dillon could. "It's nice to meet you, Rose."

"Oh, call me Charlie," Charlie said.

"All right. Dillon's told me a lot about you."

"He has?" Charlie said, looking surprised.

"Of course I did," Dillon said. "How could I not talk about the most amazing woman I've ever met?"

"I knew I'd like you. Hi, I'm Marty."

"It's a pleasure to meet you, Marty. I understand I have you to thank for bringing Charlie to Black Light. I owe you."

"Well, I'll consider the debt paid if Charlie can tell me she's not destined to spend the rest of her vacation turning into a couch potato."

Charlie laughed. "I've already told him you were right. My shoes... and everything else, were definitely knocked off."

"I knew it!" Marty said, beaming from ear to ear. "It's about damn time! Though I don't know what I'm going to do with myself not having to wait on you hand and foot."

"Don't worry, that's my job," Dillon said. "We'll get together soon, but for now..." He bent and when he straightened, he had Charlie hanging over his shoulder. "Say goodnight, Charlie."

She lifted her head. "Goodnight, Charlie," she repeated and then squealed when his hand snaked up her dress and slapped her bare butt.

"Smartass," Dillon said, giving her buttock a squeeze as he walked towards the door.

CHAPTER 6

*O*nce Danny had buzzed the locker open, and Charlie had retrieved her purse and watch, she again took Dillon's hand. Her mind was whirling with all that had happened and yet she wouldn't have changed a single moment. Looking around, and realizing they were walking down a tunnel, she said, "This isn't the way we came in."

"There's more than one secret entrance," Dillon said, squeezing her hand.

He led her up a set of stairs and through another door where a man sat. "Have a good evening. Come back soon," he said.

"Believe me, we plan on doing both," Dillon said, causing Charlie's face to heat and her panties to dampen... wait, she wasn't wearing any panties. God, she hoped that unlike Hansel and Gretel, she wasn't leaving a path to follow... though hers would be droplets of her arousal instead of breadcrumbs. That brought another wave of heat, this time throughout her entire body.

Dillon pushed aside a curtain and she stepped through, surprised to find they stood in some sort of store. If the books and paraphernalia sitting on shelves didn't give her a clue to the store's offerings, a dark haired woman sitting at a table where a large, glass ball sitting in the middle of a round table certainly did.

"A psychic shop? I've always wanted to have my future told."

Dillon halted her approach to the table. "Your immediate future will involve a tall, dark, and handsome man and though there will be balls involved, they won't be glass."

"Dillon! I can't believe you said that!" she gasped as he led her out the door. "She's going to think we are some sort of perverts!"

"Babe, if she can't tell that I intend to do all sorts of delicious perverted things to you, then she's not much of a psychic."

Charlie forgot all about the woman as his words had her stomach flipping and her naughty bits tingling. When they turned into a parking lot, she said, "You didn't come in a cab?"

Dillon chuckled. "No. Not too many cab drivers want to drive all the way out to my place without another fare to bring back into the city."

"Oh my God, Dillon, this is gorgeous!" And it was. He was unlocking the door of a cherry apple red, Chevy pick-up. "What year is it?"

"It's a 1948. We found it in an old barn on one of our trips. My dad loved restoring old trucks. It made for some great father/son bonding as he passed on his skills and knowledge. When other kids were pining for the newest, sportiest cars, we were restoring trucks. Owen has a 1956 Ford." As he was speaking, he was lifting her into the truck. Instead of the bucket seats of most of today's vehicles, she was placed on a wide seat that ran across the width of the vehicle. She was shocked at how spacious the interior was and how huge the hood looked through the curved glass of the windshield.

"I love it!" she said as he climbed behind the wheel. Reaching over her shoulder, her hand encountered nothing but empty space. "No seat belts?"

"They weren't a requirement then, especially not on what were classified as farm vehicles." He turned and grinned. "Come on over here." Once she had, he reached behind her and pulled out a belt that had been tucked into the seat. "But, as much as I appreciate vintage, I also appreciate safety first."

Charlie smiled as he buckled the belt over her lap, not surprised that he'd added them but absolutely loving that she was able to sit so close to his side. He gave her a quick kiss before he started the ignition, the engine purring to life.

"This is much better than a cab," she said, leaning her head against his shoulder. "But if you don't live in D.C., where do you live?"

"I live in Virginia."

"Isn't that a bit far?"

"Not at all. But believe me, those thirty-five miles or so take you into a different world. I've never been much for cities, crowds, and traffic. I grew up on a farm and when my parents passed, Owen and I inherited it and when he decided to move into the city, I bought his share."

Charlie smiled. "I think that's wonderful. Keep family land in the family. I've always preferred open spaces as well. Easier to see anyone sneaking up on you. Oh, Martha's place is over by the Capital. I think if you turn right at the light you can cut over to… hey, I said right."

He'd driven straight through the intersection. "Babe, we aren't going to Martha's place until much, much later."

She looked down at her watch. "It's already midnight…" She giggled and when he asked what was funny, she told him about Martha making her promise to stay out until the clock struck twelve. "I'm glad I did," she said, laying her hand on his thigh. "Instead of some carriage that turns into a pumpkin, I'm riding in a beautiful truck with…" Realizing she'd been about to say Prince Charming, she felt her cheeks heat.

Dillon's hand dropped to cover hers. "With a man who thinks you are far better than any princess."

"You do?"

"Absolutely." They'd stopped at a red light and he took the opportunity to bend to kiss her, instantly igniting the heat he'd stoked earlier. She gave a soft moan when he released her, his eyes to the front again. It gave her a moment just to stare at his profile and thank God that Martha had insisted she go out tonight. Dillon had said he owed Martha and she knew he wasn't the only one.

"So where are we going?" she asked as he drove through streets she wasn't familiar with.

"I've got this sweet little place that serves the best stack of pancakes you've ever eaten."

"That sounds great but I'm not really that hungry…"

"You will be by the time it opens."

"What time is that?"

"Whenever the chef crawls out of bed, which, could be very late."

"You know the chef?"

Dillon turned to glance at her, his smile causing that sexy dimple to appear in his cheek. "Quite well, actually. I know that since he plans on making love to a beautiful yellow Rose until the wee hours of the morning, he might be a tad bit later than usual in getting to the kitchen."

She suddenly understood what he was saying. They weren't going to Martha's nor any restaurant in D.C. He was taking her to his place. Emotions warred within her. She'd honestly never imagined anything remotely like this to be in her future. Sure, their paths might have crossed again given their professions, but to walk into a BDSM club and to not only see Dillon, but to participate in a scene… a very intense, emotional, extremely satisfying scene had never once crossed her mind as a possibility. Part of her insisted things were moving too fast and yet… her heart and, if she were honest, her body were telling her to trust that somehow the stars had aligned in her favor. At least for this one night, they encouraged her to allow herself to let go of her worries about realities of life, job, and expectations – and just enjoy.

"Charlie? Are you okay? Tell me what you're thinking?" Dillon asked softly, adding, "And remember, there are no right and wrong answers here."

This man was like no one she'd ever known. She'd been shocked to see him, had run as he advanced, had every intention of fleeing and yet had been so... so pleased when he'd not allowed her to open the door. She'd felt his erection pressing against her as he'd pinned her to the wall and yet he hadn't demanded, hadn't taken a thing until he'd taken the time to sit and talk. Oh, he was definitely the Dom in the scenario, but he'd wanted to assure her that she was in charge of whether their play progressed or ended. She had absolutely no doubt that if she asked him to take her to Martha's, he'd simply turn the truck around and do so even though they were already leaving the city behind. She made her decision, and knew it was the only one she could have made. Their night wasn't over... it was really just beginning. The promise of more to come had her body tingling again. Looking up and meeting his eyes, she smiled. "I was thinking that if breakfast is so far in the future, maybe I better have a little snack to tide me over." She unclicked her seat belt and then pulled her legs up to lie on the bench, scooting back until she was in the position she desired, before buckling the belt around her waist again. The large steering wheel was high enough that she had plenty of room to maneuver as she unzipped his pants, loving the fact that the moment he realized her intentions, his cock had begun to harden. She also loved that he went commando... making his erection so much more convenient. Guiding him out of his fly, she bent to kiss the head, then began taking tiny licks across its surface, her hand stroking his shaft as it continued to lengthen. God, she really was amazed that she'd managed to take every inch of his cock inside, the memory of being so full, so stretched, causing her pussy to spasm.

She didn't hurry, didn't jerk her hand up and down his shaft. She had an entire thirty-five miles or so and was planning on savoring every single click of the odometer. Using her tongue, she swept it from his balls to the crown, tasting him as he'd tasted her. Glistening drops of pre-cum were licked and savored, the masculine scent and taste uniquely his. Opening her mouth wide, she engulfed the bulbous head, humming with pleasure.

He was as soft as velvet and yet as hard as iron, the vein on the underside, thick and prominent beneath her tongue. Every inch of his erection felt her tongue as she alternated between taking his cockhead into her mouth and licking along his length. She began to bob her head up and down, taking a bit more every time, yet knowing it would take practice... a lot of practice, before she could discover if she'd ever be able to take all of him. Her fingers alternated between stroking and caressing that which she couldn't take.

Perhaps he was the psychic one as the moment she had that thought, he said, "More, Charlie. Take more." She managed another inch and then pulled away, only to find his hand on the back of her head. "Just like your pussy, you can take more."

Her pussy spasmed again at the memory and her nipples throbbed at the tone of his voice. It was so calm, so deep, so authoritative, and so absolutely certain that he spoke the truth. She found she wanted so desperately to obey, to please this man who had so pleased her. Another inch taken and he was now at the back of her throat and she was having to fight her gag reflex.

His hand didn't push but didn't allow her to retreat. Strong fingers wove through her hair and she realized that it didn't take ropes to bind a person. It simply took the desire to give up control to another. To offer yourself in submission, trusting your Dom never to harm you. With a deep breath, she swallowed, forcing herself to take him down her throat, forcing herself not to panic at the fear of being unable to breathe.

"Beautiful," he said, "a little more."

If someone had told her that she could actually swallow a man's cock, she would have called them a liar. And yet, with his softly spoken command, with his hand on the back of her head, and with her desire to learn, she did exactly that. Another inch and then another until she had to pull back, saliva slipping from her lips, gasping as she drew in oxygen. And yet, the moment she was only holding his cockhead in her mouth, she craved more. Again and again, she took him, swallowed around him, each contraction of her throat squeezing his flesh. When she needed to breathe, she pulled back and did so, and only realized his hand had left her head when she felt her dress being lifted.

"Spread your knees," he said, and when she did, the seat plenty wide enough to accommodate his order, she felt his fingers slip from her ass to her sex. She gasped at the pleasure as he began to stroke along her vulva as her mouth continued to slide up and down his cock. "You'll come with me," he said, not a question, nor an order. It was said as a simple fact. His fingers played over her clit and when the only sound she could make was a deep hum, she felt his cock go even harder. Two fingers slipped into her pussy, her juices allowing them easy entry. He began to finger fuck her as she increased her pace, worshipping the cock in her mouth, welcoming it down her throat.

"Come, Charlize, come for me."

It took only another few thrusts, the heel of his palm pressing hard against her clit for her to obey. She came as he spurted deep in her throat, both continuing to convulse, to release the passion they'd brought to the surface. Swallowing, she took every drop as he forced every spasm from her. When it was over, she was breathless. She allowed his cock to slip from her mouth, her lips feeling swollen. Kissing the tip again, she smiled to see his cock give a final shudder. Tucking him away, she carefully zipped his pants before giving a sigh of intense satisfaction and laying her head on his thigh, easing her legs down as his fingers left her sex.

"Open," he said, causing her to open eyes she'd just closed to find his glistening fingers. A shudder ran through her, but not one of disgust. Yes, she'd taken some classes, had played a bit but had never once felt anything like this. His simple command had a wave of submission running through her. Opening her mouth, he slid his fingers inside and as she licked and cleaned each one, she thought of how they were joined... his seed and hers, both on her tongue in what she could only describe as an intimate kiss.

When he pulled his fingers free, he stroked her hair off her face. "That was beautiful... you are beautiful." She sat up, accepting his kiss and once more snuggling into his side.

"We're almost home," he said and she realized that the city had disappeared, replaced by rolling fields. Stars filled the sky and the moon was within days of being full.

"It's so beautiful," she said. "Even in the dark, when you can't see clearly, I know that beneath the darkness, there is beauty."

They sat in comfortable silence for the last few miles before he turned off onto another road. After driving about a mile, he stopped the truck in front of a gate. Rolling down the window, he reached out and punched in a code, then drove through, the gates closing behind him. "Welcome home," he said, and she smiled at the sound of pride in his tone. They pulled up in front of a two-story house that had a large front porch. Charlie scooted across the seat, blushing and hoping that she hadn't left a wet spot on the leather. Dillon opened her door and reached in, snagging her about the waist and swinging her down.

"How much land do you have?" she asked, the moon's illumination allowing her to see nothing but fields and a few buildings typical on many farms and ranches she'd seen growing up in Texas.

"Two-thousand acres, but I lease most of them out to other farmers. My family always grew crops, but I don't really farm."

"Ah, so you're one of those 'gentlemen farmers'. The king of his domain and yet doesn't get his hands dirty."

Dillon chuckled and took her hand to lead her up the porch

steps. "Believe me, I get plenty dirty." She heard barking and smiled when Dillon called out, "Lucy, I'm home," in a perfect imitation of Desi Arnez from the *I Love Lucy* television series. At his welcome, the barking ceased.

"Your own version of an alarm system?" she asked as he pulled open the screen and unlocked the door.

"Can't beat it as it doesn't take a lick of electricity and offers a much warmer welcome."

Charlie laughed as Lucy came bounding into the foyer. She was about to brace herself for impact, but Lucy came to a smooth stop a foot from her, sitting down and lifting her head. Charlie could swear the dog was smiling as if to say, 'Really? You forgot how well trained I am?' Sinking to her knees, Charlie wrapped her arms around the German Shepherd's neck. "Hello, girl. I've missed you." Lucy gave Charlie's cheek a long sweep of her tongue and Charlie kissed her right back.

"All right, ladies," Dillon said. "I'm feeling a bit left out here."

Charlie smiled as he rectified the situation by squatting and spending a few moments ruffling Lucy's fur before he rose and offered Charlie his hand. Charlie put her hand in his, expecting him to pull her to her feet. Instead, she squealed when he not only pulled her up but then swept her into his arms in one fluid movement.

"I'll give you the grand tour tomorrow, but for now, there's only one room I'm interested in showing you."

He carried her through a large living room and then up the stairs. It was apparent he knew every step, every room by heart as he never bothered to turn on any of the lights until he pushed open a door at the end of the hallway. Once inside, he set her down and with a flick of the switch, she could take in the room. It was obviously his bedroom. A king size bed dominated the space opposite a set of windows. One wall held a large dresser, and one corner was claimed by a leather chair and ottoman. A small table set beside it, a pile of magazines testifying that this was where he'd sit and read. She wasn't the least bit surprised to see solemn looking men and women on the covers, each one with an equally serious looking canine by their side. It was a room inside a house that had stood for generations. The very thought of years past and Dillon as a baby being brought home by proud parents, that little boy growing up here, the magazines replaced by comic books, had her smiling. This wasn't a house... this was a home and she was amazed at how much that tugged on her heart. That little boy had grown up into an incredible man, one she felt safe with... one she felt honored to be with.

"I didn't see much, but I'm sure the house is lovely," she said, turning and then gasping. While she'd been looking around the room, he'd been removing his clothing. Yes, that little boy had grown up into quite the perfect male specimen. His torso was a slab of muscle, his waist trim and that dark line of hair that led from his navel down to his groin had her heart slamming inside her chest. Good God, despite coming down her throat not that long ago, his cock jutted from his groin, standing at attention and pointing in her direction. She felt a ridiculous impulse to salute and then an almost irresistible desire to sink to her knees as a wave of submission rolled over her.

His eyes locked on hers as she lifted them to his face as he came towards her. Nipples instantly puckered and her thighs grew damper when her body immediately responded to him. "Time to step out of the beautiful pumpkin," he said and she almost rolled her eyes, catching herself just in time.

"Ahh, good save," he said, smiling as he unzipped her dress, allowing it to fall to the floor. "I'm regularly tested and am clean, but will use a condom if you wish."

What she wanted was to feel his cock inside her without anything between them. "I'm clean and on birth control. So, no, Dillon. I want to feel you, and nothing but you." He enveloped her in his arms, drawing her close, and for the first time, she felt the delicious heat of all of his bare flesh against hers as he bent to kiss her. She moaned, her arms lifting to wrap around his neck as she opened her mouth for him to plunder. God, his kisses alone had her blood racing and her pussy leaking. Of course, the long length of his cock pressed between them didn't hurt either.

Not breaking the kiss, he walked her backwards until she could feel the edge of the mattress against her ass. Lifting his mouth from hers, he turned her in his arms. "Bend over, legs spread, ass high."

She immediately obeyed, laying her torso against the quilt that covered his bed, the deep greens, browns, and golds of the design as masculine as the man behind her. Her fingers grabbed hold of the quilt as she gave a cry when he impaled her with his cock in one hard thrust, filling her completely. Whereas at the club he'd taken it slow, here... now... he took her hard and fast. His foot kicked against her own, ordering her to spread herself wider, his hands on her hips lifting her ass higher as he buried himself again and again in her pussy.

"Oh... oh, God," she moaned, "yes... yes. Harder!"

His hand moved to fist in her hair, pulling her head back, turning it so that he could bend forward and claim the tender skin of her throat. It was primal, it was hard, it was fast... it was absolute perfection. She screamed his name when she came apart, every inch of her body convulsing, her cunt squeezing around his cock like a vise and yet unable to hold him in place as he continued to drive in and out of her. His hips slammed into her again and again. She didn't feel as if she were just being fucked... she felt as if he was claiming her, with his cock, his lips, his tongue, and his teeth as he took small nips on her neck, her ear, her shoulder. Her body began to coil again as she imagined how it would be to bend before him, to offer her body for his mark in a different way... to accept each stroke of his hand, his belt, a crop, a flogger. To know that beneath her clothing—he, and she—knew that the weals she bore with pride were those he'd gifted her with.

"Come for me, Charlie. Come all over my cock."

85

"Yes," she screamed as fingers pinched a clit that was so sensitive already, demanding she obey her Dom's order. She swore the stars had moved inside as she saw them explode behind her eyelids as yet another climax took her. Dillon bellowed her name, his cock jetting his seed so deeply inside her as he continued to stroke in and out for several more, long, delicious moments. When he bent over her, his weight pressing her deeper into the mattress, she didn't feel smothered, she felt incredibly protected and it felt surprisingly nice.

After he'd removed her shoes and stockings, she'd been grateful to find herself lifted into his arms again, positive she never would have had the strength to walk into the adjoining bathroom.

"Oh, this is gorgeous," Charlie said looking around the bathroom. She learned that while the farmhouse was over a hundred-years-old, Dillon had done a few upgrades. Besides the claw foot tub on one side, there was a huge walk-in shower with multiple shower heads that would not only wash but massage every inch of their bodies. Though thoroughly updated, a beautiful old piece of furniture had been converted into a vanity, and though it only held one sink, it was oversized, with a faucet on either end.

Instead of setting her on her feet, he set her down on the vanity. She was about to state she could stand but then decided it might not be a good idea to state something she was pretty sure was a lie. Not only her legs, but her entire body felt a bit wobbly. So instead, as he moved about the room gathering whatever he wanted, she leaned her head against the wall and closed her eyes.

"Charlie? Honey? Charlie?"

"Hmmm?

"Wake up, honey."

"I'm not asleep," she said.

"If you're not, you're about one second from falling into the Sandman's arms." She gave a squeak as he lifted her off the counter and carried her into the shower.

"Oh, God, that feels so good," she moaned, finally opening her eyes to see billows of steam surrounding her as jets of water pummeled her skin. When he turned her back to his front and tilted her head back in order to begin washing her hair, she groaned again. "That feels even better."

"I love what you've done with your hair." His fingers lifted a section. "The streak of color, among the black, is stunning."

"I love your hands in my hair," she said, almost purring as his fingers massaged her scalp.

He bent close, giving her shoulder a kiss. "Good to know, Charlie. I plan on having my hands in your hair quite often. To wash, to caress, to pull as you take my cock... in your mouth, your cunt, and your ass."

She shuddered at the words... positive he wasn't asking permission; he was simply telling her what he would do. That thought... no, that promise, didn't scare her. Sure, she could imagine female activists demanding she stand up for her gender, to state that he had no such rights and yet... to hell with them. What his word did instead was help her to understand a bit more about exactly why women such as she—strong, intelligent, independent women—still ached to serve that one person, to offer their submission to the one who stirred their very souls. With her hair washed, he moved to wash the rest of her, soaping his hands and running them over her breasts. When she moaned, he stopped moving, just gently holding her breasts.

"Sore?"

"A little," she admitted, reaching up to lay her palm on his cheek. "But the good type of sore."

He smiled and bent to give each of her nipples a gentle kiss. "Here too?" he asked, slipping his hand between her legs and cupping her sex.

"Yes... you're a very well-endowed man, MacAllister."

"And you are a very beautiful woman, Charlize. An amazing woman." He turned her and washed her back and the globes of her ass. She stiffened when she felt a finger sliding down the cleft of her bottom. "Relax," he ordered as the tip of his finger pressed against the tight pucker of her anus. "Have you ever been fucked here?"

"No... never." When the memory of Sorenson threatened to rear its ugly head, she forced it aside. It was yet another memory that needed to be supplanted. One that she trusted Dillon to replace over with his lovemaking... even if the thought of taking his cock into such a small place had her blushing at the very taboo nature of it.

"We'll begin working you up to being able to take my cock," Dillon said, again not questioning, just informing.

She nodded, heat filling her very blood vessels at the image that popped into her head, and when he stroked her pucker one final time before removing his finger, she knew it would be another gift she would offer to him. While he washed his hair, she washed his body, amazed when his cock began to stiffen as she lathered it with her hands.

"God, are you always hard?"

"Only around you," he said with a grin. "Shit, all that time in Texas just about killed me. I wanted you so badly but you kept saying no every time I asked you out."

She cupped his testicles, rolling them in her palm. "A girl can't appear too easy, now can she?" she quipped and then shook her head. "To be honest, I regretted not accepting a date. That last night at Lupitos, I was so torn apart knowing I'd ruined any chance of... of us." She paused, looking up at him. "God, Dillon, what are the possibilities that you'd live here and that I'd take my vacation in D.C. and that we'd both..."

"Enjoy the spicier side of life?" he provided.

She couldn't help but smile. "That's one way to put it."

He bent and kissed the top of her head. "I couldn't tell you the statistical possibility but I will tell you that I felt as if I'd won the lottery the moment I saw you at Black Light."

His words and the look in his eyes had her insides going all warm and gooey. Feeling a movement, she looked down to see that his cock was hardening. Smiling, she was amazed that he wanted her yet again. "I feel the same way, except my ticket also has the winning powerball," she said, giving his balls a gentle squeeze.

"Babe, unless you want to go beyond a little sore to a lot sore, I suggest you move your hand." When she began to stroke her hand up and down his stiffening shaft, he put his hand over hers. "Smartass." She laughed but allowed him to remove her hand as she really was about to fall asleep on her feet.

Dillon wrapped her in a towel that was huge enough to go around her twice. He settled her on the counter yet again as he plugged in a hair dryer and combed out and dried her hair until it wasn't sopping wet but still a bit damp. "It takes a long time," she said with a huge yawn. "It's really thick."

"And gorgeous," he said, putting away the dryer and handing her a toothbrush he pulled from a drawer and unwrapped. "Brush your teeth and empty your bladder."

She brushed her teeth as he did his and was grateful when he stepped from the bathroom, giving her some privacy. As she jumped down from the counter, she realized how high it was. By the time she'd flushed the toilet, he was back, scooping her off her feet yet again.

"You know, a girl could get used to this," she said as she saw that he'd turned down the bed.

"I hope so," Dillon said, sliding her between the sheets and then climbing in behind her. He snapped off the lamp and settled his arm around her waist, pulling her to spoon against him, lifting to kiss her softly. "I'll carry you around for the rest of time in thanks for looking up to see you in the club tonight."

Again his words had her breath catching in her throat and she remembered her fear when she'd realized he had seen her in a sex club. Smiling, she turned her head to look over her shoulder at him. "Even if I'm a freak?"

"You're my kind of freak... beautiful, intelligent, sexy as hell, and willing to embrace your kink."

"Hmmm, so I'm a kinky freak." She yelped when he popped her bare ass.

"No, you're a smartass kinky freak. Now, close your eyes and sleep. The sun comes up early."

"So? I thought we were going to sleep in?"

"You surprise me. I'd think a gal from Texas would know chores come early on a farm."

Charlie groaned and pushed tighter against him and snuggled deeper into the pillow, falling into sleep before he even finished speaking.

CHAPTER 7

*C*harlie jerked awake and squealed, barely able to close her mouth in time before a broad rough tongue swept across her face again. Pushing the heavy, furry body away, she squirmed to sit up. "Lucy, no!" she scolded, wiping her hand over the wet path the dog's tongue had left. Lucy simply plopped down and put her head on Charlie's lap.

"Don't blame her," Dillon said. "Every time I tried to wake you, you just grumbled and turned over. You are definitely not a morning person, Charlie."

Squinting her eyes, she looked towards the windows. "Is it even morning?"

He chuckled. "For several hours now. You must have missed the cock's crow."

Running her gaze over him, she said, "Unless I've suddenly started having very explicit dreams, I'm pretty sure I was awakened to the man with the cock crowing in the middle of the night."

Dillon grinned. "Complaining?"

"Not at all," Charlie said, leaning towards him as he sat on the edge of the bed, accepting his kiss.

He pulled away and kissed her forehead. "Good job, Lucy. I do think our girl is finally awake."

"How come I smell coffee but no bacon?" Charlie asked, sniffing the air.

"Because farmers don't eat before they take care of their stock. But, you can have a cup of coffee if you'll get out of that bed."

"Isn't it a crime to bribe an officer of the law?" Charlie teased, but allowed him to pull the covers down.

"I don't think that applies to coffee, smartass," he said, picking up the clothes he'd laid at the end of the bed. "Put these on and I'll lead you to the coffee pot."

She reached for the clothes and then paused. "Um, underwear?"

"Your panties are in the wash, as is your dress."

"And my bra?" she asked, somehow not the least bit surprised to learn he had been thoughtful enough to do her laundry.

"Hmm, it's not here?" he asked, lifting the t-shirt as if expecting to find it beneath. "No? Lucky me, I guess that means you'll go commando."

She rolled her eyes and reached for the shirt. "I thought that only referred to… panties or briefs."

"Well, in your case, it applies to sexy bras as well," he said, reaching to caress her breasts and plucking at her nipples.

She smiled and when he pulled back, held up the t-shirt. "This looks way too small for you."

"That's because it's Janet's," he said, grinning. "Janet is known to leave clothing scattered all over the county. I bet there's not a farm within a fifty-mile radius that doesn't have a few changes of clothing lying around. She's a very popular young woman." When she looked at him, his grin faded as he saw the brightness in her eyes dimming. Shit, he had meant to tease… not hurt or cause her to suddenly have awkward 'morning after' thoughts.

He pulled her to him. "Hey, I'm just teasing. I've known Janet since she was a baby. She's a great girl who pitches in wherever needed and with a few additional, as you call us, gentlemen farmers, she is in demand. She makes enough money to pay her way through college and has earned enough experience she hopes to be a shoo-in for veterinary school." Though he certainly hadn't expected it, he couldn't blame Charlie when she slapped his chest.

"Have you no shame, MacAllister? You painted her as some sort of fantasy farmer's daughter every man within miles lusts after."

"Yeah, that was pretty awful but I promise, I really didn't mean to disparage her or upset you, Charlie. In fact, Janet is a bit like you. Knows what she wants and doesn't let anything stand in her way."

"I admire women who find a way to make their dreams come true. Maybe I'll give her a few pointers on self-defense," Charlie said.

Dillon chuckled. "With five brothers, I'm pretty sure she's got that covered and if she knew I teased you like that, I'm pretty sure they'd stand by and encourage her to flip me on my ass."

"Good, I think I'm going to like this girl." She stood up on her tiptoes and brushed his cheek with her lips and then stepped back and began to pull the t-shirt over her head. Muffled words came from beneath the fabric. "Um, exactly how large is Janet?"

The reason for her question became obvious as her head popped through the neck opening, and her breasts flattened beneath the too tight fabric.

"Well, she's tall but obviously far less curvaceous than that fictional farmer's daughter bombshell. Here, let me help." He tugged the shirt off and walked to his dresser, returning with one of his own shirts. It swallowed Charlie whole but at least she'd be able to breathe. She pulled on the jeans and watched as they promptly slid from her hips.

"Hold up, I can take care of that as well."

"Dillon, there is no way your pants will fit me," Charlie said, bending to tug the jeans back up.

"Hold your shirt up," he ordered as he returned again from his dresser. She used one hand to obey and the other kept the jeans from falling again. He pushed a white rope through the loops and then tugged the ends until the waist drew in.

"You just happen to have shibari ropes lying around?"

"Yes. I practice tying knots and different patterns," he said, tying the ends of the rope, bending forward to kiss her stomach, before tugging her shirt down. "Besides, it will make me happy to know that you're wearing a rope that will one day be tied about your body in a different way."

Dillon knelt to roll the cuffs of the jeans up and then handed her the first sneaker. When it became obvious it was too big, he sat back on his heels. "You can't go barefoot outside, but I don't think your heels would survive."

"Give me a pair of your socks," she said, removing the shoe. Once he had, the additional thickness allowed the shoe to fit snugger and she tightened the laces. Standing, she looked down at herself. "Not exactly ready for the runway, but thank you."

"You look adorable," he said. "Ready for some coffee?"

"Absolutely."

Once in the kitchen, he pressed the mug he prepared into her hands, smiling as she inhaled deeply and gave a moan as she took the first sip. "God, I will never tire of hearing that sound. Whether it's when drinking coffee, eating some sinful dessert, or sucking my cock." She lifted her gaze, the rim of the mug at her lips as color began to creep up her neck to stain her cheeks. "I love that blush, too."

She had the mug empty within a few minutes, her head tilting to one side. "Do I hear dogs?"

"You do," Dillon agreed. "Come meet my stock."

When they stepped out the kitchen door, she said, "The porch wraps around the whole house?"

"Yes, and its width helped keep the house cool in the summer before Dad put in central air and heat." They walked hand-in-hand down the steps and across the yard towards a large barn. When he opened a gate, she stopped.

"Wow, this is amazing. You train dogs here, don't you?"

Dillon saw her looking around the enclosed area. There were areas designated to teach dogs that would become K-9 partners different skills. Large round cylinders snaked around the yard, narrow boards made little bridges, sets of bars at various levels stood waiting to have a dog climb over or crawl beneath.

"Well, they start their training here. By the time they are old enough to be matched with their eventual owner, they finish their training at Quantico right alongside their human partner."

"I loved watching the teams working together when you were in Texas. People see drug dogs at places like the airport, but aren't really aware of how much training they go through.

"That's true," Dillon said. "The dogs' training starts young before they ever meet their partners. In fact, I've got a group within days of earning their certification. You can come with me and watch, if you'd like."

"Really? I'd love that."

"It's a date," he said, squeezing her hand. "But first, we've got chores to do, young lady. Ready?"

"Yes, Sir!" she practically shouted.

They entered the barn to the sound of excited barking and the sight of dogs of various ages. Charlie slapped her hands over her ears as Dillon gave a piercing whistle. Her jaw dropped as the cacophony instantly was silenced. "Wow," she said, removing her hands.

"Like I said, their training starts early." He showed her where the food was and she worked beside him to fill the many bowls. "Their water runs through pipes and is always on," Dillon explained as he squatted down beside her. "They are fed twice a day—in the morning and evening. That's one thing that Janet helps with. When I was in Texas, she stayed here at the house so she could not only take care of them but run them through their training. It's important not to disrupt their regimen for too long a time. I honestly don't know how I'm going to get along without her when she is accepted into vet school. I've counted on her for years. All I have to do is call and say I'm running late, and she runs over to feed them and just play a bit."

"Play, now that's what I'm talking about," Charlie said, rubbing the tummy of the puppy who'd rolled over onto his back. "They are so adorable!"

Dillon grinned and shook his head. "You're like Janet —spoiling them."

"You can't spoil a puppy," she said, ruffling another's fur. "They need love just as much as humans do."

"That's true," he admitted, standing and looking around. "All right, troops, ready to play?"

Once he'd opened all the doors, the dogs poured out to follow them into the yard. Dillon made some sort of hand signal and the dogs scattered, racing around. "They need to run off some energy before any serious training begins." He picked up a large bucket and offered it to her.

"Ah, so there really were balls involved in my future," she teased, taking two of the tennis balls.

He chuckled, loving the fact that she could be so incredibly serious when needed and yet allow herself to tease and just have fun. Even in her mismatched, borrowed clothing, she looked gorgeous. She drew back her arm and threw the ball. Dogs chased after it and they spent a half hour tossing balls and praising dogs as they retrieved them, Charlie giving each one a hug before sending another ball flying.

"How on earth do you ever let them go?" she asked as they took a break. "I'm already in love with every single one."

"It helps knowing that they are going to men and women who will not only love them, but depend on them. As much as I feel I have a bond with each one that I raise or train, the bond is nothing compared to the one between the human and his K-9 partner."

"Like you and Lucy," Charlie said, rubbing her hand through Lucy's fur. The dog had come to join them, not to run around but just to sit on the sidelines like a proud mother watching her kids play.

"Yes. She's a great friend. I trust her as much if not more than anyone I've ever worked with." He too gave the dog a pat and then said, "Great, come meet Janet."

He introduced the two women and then watched as they started chatting as if they'd known each other all their lives. While some women would have been uncomfortable having to even explain why they weren't wearing their own clothes, Charlie thanked Janet for the use of hers. He wasn't the least bit surprised to hear Charlie asking if Janet had applied to the veterinary program at A&M.

"Yes, but it's one of the hardest to get into," Janet said.

"I'm an alumnus of the university and have some contacts. I'd be glad to help and put in a good word for you if you'd like," Charlie offered and Janet's squeal and hug told of her excitement.

Dillon ran a few of the younger pups through some exercises, while Janet showed Charlie some commands that would direct the older ones through some paces. They worked for another hour before Dillon called a halt. "I'm starving. How about those pancakes I promised?"

"And bacon," Charlie reminded. "And more coffee. Janet, can you join us?"

"No, but thanks. I've already eaten. I'll finish up here and then I have to run out to the Adams' place. Their mare is about to foal and Doc Worchel is going to let me do the exam."

Dillon took Charlie back to the house, refusing her offer to help him cook. "Just sit there and keep me company," he said, pouring her another cup of coffee. They continued to talk about the dogs and the training until he set a huge stack of pancakes on the table, adding another plate of bacon.

"Do you have any other stock?" she asked as she poured a generous amount of syrup over her pancakes.

"We have some horses," Dillon said, sliding a couple of pieces of bacon onto her plate. "They aren't as patient with furry things nipping at their feet as people are. The stables are not far from here and they have their own pastures. Do you ride?"

"I do," she said. "I have since as long as I can remember."

"Good, then we'll add a horseback ride to our agenda. Oh, did you have something else planned?"

Charlie shook her head and ate her last piece of bacon after dipping it into a pool of syrup. "Let me think. Um, I could either get blisters walking around and staring up at some cold, marble statues, or ride with a warm, blooded, very much alive man... nope, no plans. I'm all yours to command for as long as you want me."

Dillon knew she was teasing but the words were music to his ears. He stood and moved behind her chair, bending over to kiss her, his hands cupping her breasts, rubbing his thumbs over her nipples that instantly puckered. "In that case, young lady, through there and down the stairs, you'll find a door." He nodded towards a door across the way. "I command you to be kneeling naked beside it by the time I put the dishes in the dishwasher."

She moaned and his cock twitched. Giving her earlobe a nip, he pulled her up and swatted her behind. "And I load fast!"

"Yes, Sir," she said softy.

Dillon watched as she walked to the door to the basement and though she'd obviously been aroused, had instantly obeyed his order, he saw her hesitate for a moment. She looked back and he said nothing, just gave her a smile, grateful that it seemed to be enough assurance for her to open the door and disappear down the stairs.

Though he'd spoken the truth about being quick, he took his

time, allowing her some space to settle and himself a few minutes to simply think. He'd known about his proclivities since a young age, probably even younger than most as his brother Owen had the same desires of playing on a deeper level than most couples. He'd been attracted to Charlie from the moment he'd met her in Texas but she'd done an exceptional job of hiding her submissive nature behind her tough exterior. The very fact that she'd gone undercover in the role of a woman at a party where the play could become rough had only strengthened his belief that she was a strong woman. But, he'd also seen her eyes and for the first time, had understood that Charlize Fullerton was not as hard as she might wish people to think. Though the bruises he'd seen had made his blood boil, they weren't what had given him a clue that she was struggling with the role she'd been asked to play. He'd seen her eyes, the look in them—the warrior battling with the woman. Her eyes had giving him his first inkling that beneath the surface, Charlie was craving something... someone who would take the time to peel back all those layers she'd built up over the years.

Last night, at Black Light, he'd witnessed the true submissive woman begin to emerge from inside Charlize Fullerton. He'd watched her eyes soften and her body responding to his every command, his every touch. Washing the iron skillet he'd used, he was surprised at the stab of jealousy he felt. Not because of Sorenson—no, as far as he was concerned, that man was nothing but a sadistic bastard. What had him pausing as he worked was picturing her with another man, and while he was no beginner, he found he wanted to be the one—the only one—who made her tremble with the desire to serve. It was a new feeling and yet one that he knew was right. Charlie was the most amazing woman he'd ever met. As he looked towards the basement, he envisioned her nude and kneeling, waiting, wondering both what was behind the door and what he had planned once he took her through it. Her nipples would be tight and her pussy leaking, her blood pulsing through her veins and her heart beating a little faster. Fuck! Just picturing her had his cock rock hard. Closing the door on the dishwasher, he told Lucy to stay and then descended the stairs.

He found her exactly as he'd ordered. Last night she'd said that she hadn't much experience with the many possibilities of the BDSM world. But, looking at her now, he understood that she'd paid attention in the classes she'd taken. Her very pose stated she'd had at least some basic training in submissive positions. Charlie was in the 'rest' or 'waiting' position. She was sitting with her legs tucked beneath her so her butt rested on her heels. Her hands were placed palms up on her thighs which were slightly apart, and her head was lowered. And like he'd imagined, her nipples were tightly puckered little berries, but as for her sex, he'd need a better look. "Spread your thighs wider. I want to be able to see your glistening pussy." She immediately shifted her legs apart and, sure enough, he could see the slickness coating the petals of her sex.

He entered the code on the electronic pad next to the door to the playroom, and when the lock clicked open, he saw Charlie give a small jerk. Anticipation was quite the aphrodisiac, he thought, as he pushed the door open and said, "Follow me."

She moved to her feet with a fluidity that told of practice. He entered the room, flipping open a panel next to the door and turning on the lights. Once she was fully inside, he closed the door behind them, hearing the lock engage, ensuring their privacy. She stood, her legs apart, her hands at her sides.

He stepped around her, reached for her arms and pulled them behind her. "When standing, I prefer for you to have your arms behind you, hands on opposite elbows. And, Charlie, while some Doms require their submissive to keep their head and eyes lowered, I love to watch the expressions on your face and look into your gorgeous eyes. Head up and face forward." Once she lifted her head, he wrapped his arms around her. "Welcome to my playroom. Go ahead, look around."

Her head slowly swiveled and he allowed her body to translate her thoughts to him. As her eyes traveled over the various areas and apparatus, he felt her breathing quicken. Her head stilled when she saw the leather swing hanging in one corner and she gave a small gasp when she moved on to see a spanking bench in another. The large St. Andrew's cross brought a soft moan, though the fact that he'd begun to roll her nipples between his fingers might have accounted for that as well. His cock stiffened as he anticipated seeing her in every possible pose—bound on, bent over, or laid across the items he'd selected with such care. He smiled as he asked himself where to start and then left the decision to her.

"What would you like to try first?" he asked.

"The swing, please."

The hesitancy was gone and he smiled. "Perfect choice," he agreed, kissing up the side of her neck to nibble on an ear. "Go kneel by the swing." He released her, pleased to see she kept her arms behind her as she went to obey his instruction. Once there, she turned to face him, sinking gracefully into the first position, only then moving her arms, laying her hands on her thighs, her fingers once more gently curled as if offering them to be bound if her Dom so desired, or to accept an object that he'd chosen to use on her body. She made a beautiful picture of supplication.

Dillon removed his boots, socks and t-shirt, leaving his pants on. He adjusted the temperature, not wanting her to become chilled. Walking across the room towards her, he saw her tongue come out and lick across her lips. He didn't stop until he was right in front of her, pleased when she lifted her head to meet his eyes.

"You've got the sexiest mouth I've ever seen. Every single time you lick those pouty little lips, all I can imagine is your tongue on my cock. Open."

She opened her mouth as he unzipped his pants and released

his erection. Sliding his fingers through her hair, he gave a slight tug, silently instructing her to her knees. "Keep your legs spread while you suck," he ordered as he pushed his cock between her lips. She immediately began to swirl her tongue across his flesh, lapping up the pre-cum that had already begun to ooze from the slit in his cock. He gave her time to taste, to lick, to kiss and then moved forward again, pushing more of his cock into her mouth. "Take more," he said, and she instantly moved down his length, taking as much as she could until he hit the back of her throat.

"Eyes," he said, reminding her that he wished to watch every expression. "Do you have any idea how fucking beautiful you look? Kneeling before me, your lips stretched around my cock, offering me the gift of your submission?" He watched her eyes soften and the flush he loved suffuse her cheeks. "Put your arms behind your back and keep them there." She did and he tightened his grip on her hair as he began to push deeper into her throat. God it was so fucking incredible, watching her body struggle against her heart's need to submit, to open her throat, to accept his cock. Every swallow was like a caress, every line of spittle leaking from her lips a beautiful symbol of her submission. This wasn't like the night before when she'd suckled his cock. No, this was him fucking her throat. Her eyes watered and she gagged but never attempted to pull away, accepting his dominance, his control. With a final push, he buried himself fully, not an inch of his shaft left for her to swallow. His cock jerked as he shot his release down her throat, her swallows milking every drop from him. Pulling back, her breasts were heaving as she drew in oxygen her shallow breaths hadn't allowed. When he pulled from her mouth, he reached down and lifted her, crushing her against his chest as he cut off her breath again with his mouth. She was so soft, so giving, so absolutely perfect.

Releasing her, he held her close until her breathing evened and then bent and lifted her into his arms and placed her on the black leather straps that made up the swing. Her hands reached to find a hold, giving a small squeak of surprise as the swing moved beneath her. He grinned and bent to kiss her again. "Lie back and just relax. You are perfectly safe." She nodded and he added, "Baby, you don't need to be silent unless instructed. I won't know if you have any questions or how you are enjoying… well, that's not true. I can see your enjoyment in your hard nipples and the wetness on your thighs. Still, I love your voice. Any questions?"

"Just one… is this what it feels like to be suspended?"

"You mean like Angelica?"

"Well, sort of. I mean, I know there were only ropes around her, but I feel suspended… at least a little."

Dillon smiled wondering if he'd smiled so much in his lifetime. "Actually, this is a good start. You need to learn to trust that I won't allow you to fall… whether that be using the swing or ropes. Now, lie back, baby."

"Oh, right," she said, lying back and wiggling a bit as if to either find a more comfortable position against the straps or to test their support. Either was fine with him. As was the laughter she gave when he pulled the swing towards him and then let it go, setting her in motion. "This is just so cool."

He chuckled as he gathered a few items and then stopped the motion of the swing. "Let's see if we can move from cool to hot, shall we?" He ordered her to lift her arms and reach above her as high as she could. Once she had, he bound her arms to the leather, making sure he wove a simple yet pretty pattern as she was such a fan of rope work. With her arms secure, he bent to kiss her and then moved to the other end of the swing.

"Pull your legs up and then open as wide as you can." When she hesitated, he said, "Let me see that gorgeous, wet cunt. Legs up and open now."

She drew her legs up and spread them, but nowhere near wide enough, but he'd take care of that. Taking her left leg, he pushed it further back and then bound it to the swing. By the time he repeated the process on her right leg, she was splayed wide, her hands almost able to grab her ankles as she was bent at a sharp angle. "Comfy?" he asked, looking down at her. He didn't have to wonder if she was a bit embarrassed as her face was pink as she nodded, but neither did he have to wonder if she was aroused. She was positively dripping. Bending, he ran his tongue up her sex, swirling his tongue around her clit that was standing so tall and proud out of its little hood. Pulling a stool up, he took a seat and began to play. He'd push her away and she'd squeal each time he pulled her back as his tongue took another taste. Each swing was gentle and soon, her little squeaks turned into moans as he'd hold her steady and nibble, lick, and suckle her clit before letting her go again. He took her to the edge over and over until she was pleading.

"Please... please, Dillon... you're... you're killing me!" Her next sound was a yelp when he swatted her upturned ass.

"How do you address me?"

"Oh... Sir, I meant, please, Sir, you're killing me!"

He chuckled, loving the fact that even with her correction of the proper address, she could still be snarky when so aroused she thought she'd die. And she would. He planned on having her experience *la petite mort,* the little death of such bliss that she'd lose consciousness of her reality for even the briefest moment. But not yet... no, she'd be begging so much more sweetly before he allowed her to fall into the abyss. The next time he brought her close, his tongue came out again... not to lick her cunt but to rim around the puckered little hole exposed by the wide spread of her legs.

"Oh my God!" she said, her attempt to scoot away impossible due to her bonds. He continued to rim her anus, and she continued to leak her arousal. He sent her swinging away again and again, alternating between her cunt and her pucker, never letting her guess the pattern, but never failing to have her gasp when his tongue found her sweet back hole. As he swung her away again, he reached for an item on the tray he'd prepared. This time when she returned, he slid the item into her pussy, insertion made easy by her arousal. She moaned with pleasure as he thrust it in and out, her hips attempting to lift as if seeking more and whined when he pulled it free.

Pushing her away again, he asked, "Do you want your little toy back?"

"Yes… yes, please, Sir."

"So sweetly asked," he said, pulling her to him. "How could I refuse?" He pushed it into her pussy again but didn't fuck her with it. Instead, he left it, her pussy walls holding it in place while he clicked open a bottle and dribbled some lube on his fingertips.

"Ohhh!" she exclaimed as he transferred some of the lube from his fingertips to her anus, circling the tight hole until it was glistening, then slowly pressing his index finger inside.

"Ohhh, ohhh, God," she moaned, as he watched her cunt spasm around the toy and another dribble of cream drip onto the floor.

"So beautiful, so perfect," he praised, bending to kiss her inner thigh. His finger breached her muscle, drawing another squeal and another drop of cream. His lips continued to kiss along the sensitive skin of her thighs as he slowly sank his finger to the hilt inside her ass. When he began to move it in and out, she groaned and he smiled as her hips were attempting to shift towards him as if asking for more.

"Oh, please…" she said as he slid his finger free and pulled the toy from her pussy.

"Please what?" he asked, as he took the time to add a coating of lube to the plug despite the wetness her own body had provided. Once it was glistening, he placed it at her virgin entrance, pressing just the slightest. "Answer me, Charlie. What do you want?"

"Oh… God…"

He believed her sense of hesitancy was not caused by her lack of desire, her very craving, but spoke of her embarrassment at asking for something she considered taboo. It was time to teach her that nothing they enjoyed together was shameful, and no part of her body wasn't his to plunder.

"Ask me for it, Charlie. Ask me to put this plug in your ass."

"I- I..."

When she continued to allow her mind to override her desire, he said, "You are more than ready, Charlie. This is just a little plug to begin training your ass to open. It's not much bigger than my finger that I slid inside your gorgeous ass. It was so hot, so tight, so beautiful." As he spoke, he kept the plug at her pucker, rubbing it around the small opening.

"Please... please put it in..."

"In where, baby?" He gave the plug a little more pressure, and yet it was only the promise of being filled as he didn't press it inside.

"In my ass. Please, Sir, please put it in my ass."

"Good girl," he praised, "Push down, baby." It took her a moment, but he saw her obey, her pucker opening just the slightest. He began to press it inside, loving every mew, every gasp, every soft cry his actions drew from her. "That's it, open up and swallow your toy." He continued to push in and withdraw until her first ring of muscle loosened. Adding a bit more pressure, he bent forward and kissed her pussy, flicking his tongue over her clit as he continued to insert the butt plug. Her sharp cry as he breached her inner ring was followed by a deep moan as he suckled on her clit. Pulling back, he seated the plug completely inside her, turning it a bit, the flange assuring it would remain exactly where it was until he chose to remove it. "You look so beautiful with your toy in your ass and your pussy pulsing."

"Please, Sir, please let me come. I'm begging you."

Dillon was proud of her acceptance of the plug and loved the sound of need in her voice. "Come for me, baby." Bending, he drew her clit into his mouth and suckled hard. His hands kept the swing still as he feasted on her core. She screamed and bucked as best she could but he kept suckling, dropping one hand to take the flange of her plug between his fingers, fucking her ass with the toy until her entire body tensed for an instant before her cry filled the room. Pushing the plug home again, he stood, locked the swing into place, pushed away the stool and buried his cock into her pussy while she continued to contract from her second orgasm.

"Oh God, oh God, oh God," she repeated as he pistoned his hips forward and back, filling her and withdrawing completely each time, her body twitching and convulsing as he fucked her. Bending forward between her splayed legs, he added licks and little bites to her nipples as she continued her mantra while climbing to the precipice. He quickened her ascent as he again began to fuck her ass with the plug... the combined sensations soon drawing the loudest cry of all as she imploded, her body shuddering, her cunt gripping his cock and her anal muscle holding the toy tightly. He thrust a final time, his voice following hers as he came. He smiled to see her head lolling, her eyes closed. Yes, his submissive had just found the sweet little death of absolute bliss.

CHAPTER 8

*W*hen she roused, it was to find she was no longer bound to the swing. In fact, she wasn't even in the playroom. Instead, she was lying back against Dillon's solid chest and his arms were wrapped around her as the tub filled.

Despite the warmth of the water and the heat of the man holding her so close, she shivered. When he'd first given her the order to go downstairs, to kneel, to wait for him, she'd felt a rush of doubt run through her, clouding the cloak of arousal that he'd already begun to wrap her in. She was falling fast... faster than she ever believed possible and that scared her a bit. What if she was the only one feeling this way? Was she the only one to feel hope that this could develop into something beyond special... something extraordinary? It had taken her a moment to banish her doubt and accept her need to find those answers. She had no problem accepting that Dillon wouldn't hurt her... at least not physically. It was her heart she was concerned about. But, she'd never find the truth unless she took a chance. And she'd been right. He had pushed her limits but, God, it had been amazing. She groaned and turned her head to look up at him. "Thank you.

That was... that was the most incredible thing I've ever experienced."

He bent and kissed her. "I'm glad you enjoyed it... several times in fact." She felt her face heat at the memory of splintering apart several times.

"God, don't you ever stop doing that."

"What, passing out from the best sex I've never even imagined was possible?"

"No, well... yes, but I meant don't ever stop blushing. I love watching the color bloom in your breasts and move up to stain your cheeks pink."

Smiling, she reached up to stroke his cheek. "I can absolutely assure you that won't be a problem as long as you, Sir, continue to do the things you do so very well."

He bent to kiss her. "Then my life will be full of pretty blushes for I certainly don't intend to stop."

Charlie felt her heart hitch. He'd said things like that before, said he'd spend the rest of time holding her... could that be true? This man had become her friend months ago but in the last two days, had become her lover, her dominant, and as she'd feared, was quickly becoming her very heart. She lived in Texas... he in Virginia. So many miles apart that it made her ache to think of them.

"Charlie, you okay?"

"Yes, I'm just a little tired."

"Then let's get you washed and tucked into bed. You didn't get much sleep last night."

"Neither did you," she said as he held her tightly to him and then reached to turn off the taps.

"Come to think of it, you're absolutely right. Guess that means I'll have to take a nap too." He reached for a washcloth and squirted some bath gel onto it. "Bend forward." She did and he began to run the sudsy cloth over her shoulders and her back. As he bathed her, turning her to face him, she began to return the favor, running her hands over his chest and then dipping beneath the water to wash his cock.

Charlie smiled when his cock twitched in her palm, deciding that she wouldn't waste time thinking of the future. No, she'd live one moment at a time, each one imprinting this man in her heart.

No matter how often she'd tried to take a nap, she'd never been very successful. She'd crawl into bed, or stretch out on the couch, close her eyes and instantly begin chastising herself for being a slugabug. Lists of things needing doing would scroll through her head until she'd abandon any attempt of catching a few winks. So, when she opened her eyes and saw that three hours had passed, she was shocked. She gave a soft purr as she felt fingers lightly tracing down her arm.

"Feel better?"

She turned and smiled, looking into the most gorgeous chocolate brown eyes she'd ever seen. "I don't see how I could ever feel better. I've never been able to just let go and fall asleep in the middle of the day."

"I've had the pleasure of watching you let go several times now and obviously you've forgotten the basic rule of napping every kid learns in kindergarten."

"And that is?"

"Choose a buddy and never nap alone." He bent to kiss her and then chuckled when the sound of her rumbling stomach was heard. "And since snacks always followed a nap, let's go raid the kitchen."

Charlie wanted to protest, but when her stomach growled again, she had to admit that food sounded good. The clothes she'd borrowed from Janet had been left in the playroom so she pulled on yet another one of Dillon's t-shirts and added a new pair of socks. He pulled on only a pair of jeans which was absolutely fine with her. After she helped him make sandwiches, they took them and tall glasses of iced-tea outside and settled into a porch swing to enjoy their lunch.

They talked about random things as they finished their meal. After he'd set their plates on a table next to the swing, he draped his arm around her shoulders, pulling her closer and she purred, feeling contentment she'd never experienced before.

"This is nice," she said, tucking her legs up on the swing and leaning into him. "It is so quiet and so beautiful here." Dillon bent to kiss the top of her head, a gesture she was finding she really enjoyed.

"More beautiful since you are here," he said. "Charlie, there's something I've been meaning to ask. Why wouldn't you go out with me when we were in Texas?"

"I did go out with you. God, I probably put on ten pounds from all the chips and enchiladas I ate at Lupitos."

"Meals out before or after work don't count. I mean this—the two of us—feels so perfect that it makes me want to kick myself for not making a pest of myself until I wore you down."

Charlie knew she could give him some quick answer that would more than likely be accepted, but knew it wouldn't be the truth. Nor would it allow her to discover the answers she sought. For that, she'd need to be completely honest, no matter how much strength it took to do so. With the heat of his body against hers, his arm holding her close and the gentle sway of the swing, she told him the truth. "I was afraid."

"Afraid? Of me?"

"No, well, not exactly… not physically. I felt so pulled towards you from the moment we met. I was afraid that if we dated, if it turned out you were as attracted to me as I was you, then when… if… the sting…"

"Went south?" he offered when she paused. "Babe, you can't allow thoughts of 'what if' to rule your life. If it went bad, we would have worked through it together."

"That's not what I mean," Charlie said and then dropped her legs and pushed up to sit. "You saw me as a fellow agent, a trained officer who could be your temporary partner. We worked together every day for months, and yes, I wanted to go out with you that first time you asked." She paused again and shook her head. "Dillon, I knew what the job required when they asked me to go undercover. I knew that it would mean I'd have to play the part of a whore..." When he reached for her, she shook her head and stood, moving to the porch railing. "People see me as some tough ass bitch. My job required that, and to be honest, I needed that perception in order to work with some of the toughest, well-trained men in law enforcement. But what they don't see, what I kept hidden, was that I've always known I was submissive. Hell, I could flip a man over my shoulder, I know how to defend myself physically, but emotionally... that's a different story. I was prepared to do whatever was necessary to get Sorenson and his men... even if that included whoring myself out."

She jerked a little when arms wrapped around her, attempting to pull away but they only tightened. "But I knew that if we dated and I fell for you as hard as I thought I would... If you saw me being that... I don't know, that I'd never forgive myself, be ashamed for being that whore."

"Oh, Charlie, you have nothing to be ashamed of. Not a goddamned thing."

She closed her eyes, remembering that night and how he'd stood before her. She'd promised herself she'd tell him the truth and dug deep yet again to do so. "Dillon, I saw your eyes. I saw the disgust in them when you saw me naked... saw the bruises..."

"Disgust? Oh, no, honey. God, I was never disgusted with you. Yes, I was angry... hell, I was fucking furious! But Charlie, not because of anything you'd done. I wanted to kill Sorenson for hurting you." He turned her, pressing her head against his chest. "You are the most incredible woman I've ever known. I respect your abilities, your determination, and, honey, I am so very sorry that I didn't hold you like this that night... didn't tell you then how very much I admire your bravery." He kissed her hair again, speaking against the ebony tresses. "What you did does not diminish you in any way. It doesn't make me think less of you. It makes me feel even more blessed that you walked into Black Light and that fate gave me a chance to make it right."

She felt the last of her shame slip away, finally understanding that it was only herself who had let shame consume her in the first place. This man was not judging her... was not condemning her for doing her job. Lifting her head, she met his eyes. "I think I knew that when you sent that text and when we finished the case, but... it took me a while to really accept that I'm not..."

"If you say freak, I'm going to bend you over this railing and blister your butt." His grin took the threat away as he bent closer. "Though, I suppose I should give you a free pass this once because, babe, I'm just as big a fan of kink as you..."

"Thank God," she said.

"Only one free pass, young lady."

She smiled. "I was actually thanking god that you are as kinky as I am."

"Ahh," he said, and her heart skipped a beat as that sexy as hell eyebrow quirked again. "Babe, you have only just begun to see how kinky I can be... how kinky we can be together." She shuddered at the look of promise in his eyes for a moment before his mouth took hers. When he let her go, she was breathless.

The sound of a ring tone pulled them apart. "That's Martha. I can't believe I haven't even thought about checking in!"

"I put your phone on the counter," Dillon said, leading her back into the kitchen and pointing to the phone. "Tell her hi for me."

Charlie picked up the phone. "Hello, Martha. How nice of you to call."

"Cut the Emily Post crap. Are you all right? God, I still can't believe what happened! It's like the stars aligned or something. If you hadn't come to D.C., if I hadn't dragged your ass to Black Light, you wouldn't have seen Dillon and I'd be rubbing your feet! Please tell me you're as good as I think you are."

Charlie laughed and took a seat on a bar stool. "I'm probably about a thousand times better than you think I am. Oh, Dillon says to tell you hello."

"Tell him hello back. Charlie, your voice sounds different, like you're really happy."

Charlie smiled, another truth coming to light. "I am. Very happy... God, I can't remember ever feeling like this. Dillon is just so..."

"Incredible, handsome, sexy..." Dillon yelled as he came back into the kitchen.

"Not to mention humble," Charlie added, smiling even as she shook her head.

"I'm so happy for you, sweetie. Look, I'm not trying to butt in or anything, I was just calling to tell you that I've left a key for you with Mrs. Evans. She's in the townhouse next to mine and is a real nice lady, but does tend to talk your ear off. Anyway, I meant to give it to you earlier but forgot."

"Okay, thanks. I'm not sure of our plans but could use some of my own clothes." Seeing Dillon gesturing, she said, "Hang on a sec."

"You're still coming out to Quantico with me tomorrow, right?"

"I'd love to."

"Good, see if Martha is free tonight. I'd love to have her join us for dinner and we can grab whatever you need."

Charlie was about to relay the question, when Martha's voice came over the phone. "I'd love to but is it all right if I ask Owen to join us? We sort of made arrangements to grab a bite before his shift begins at the club."

"Hold on. I'm sure it's not a problem, but let me ask him." Looking up, she relayed Martha's request and when Dillon began to rattle off a response, she shook her head and offered him the phone. "You can tell her yourself."

Dillon took the phone from Charlie when she offered it. "Hey,

Martha, yes, that will be even better. Call Owen and have him choose a restaurant. We'll be leaving before long so there is plenty of time to meet up and enjoy dinner before he goes to work." He paused, evidently listening to something Martha said, a grin on his face. "I will. Okay, here's Charlie."

The women only spoke for a couple of minutes before Charlie hung up. He'd brought in her dress and underwear from the laundry room.

"You will what?" she asked.

"I will remember how very incredible you are and to make you happy."

Charlie felt her face heat again, wondering how she could have possibly forgotten that Martha was... well, Martha. "Oh, good grief, I'm sorry. Sometimes Martha acts like—"

"A friend who loves you very much," Dillon completed the sentence for her. "And, she's right. Now, as much as I love seeing you in nothing but my shirt, I'm guessing you might want to change for dinner."

"Dinner? We just ate lunch!"

"Then I suppose we need to work up an appetite, don't you?" They both went upstairs to change, his projected time line delayed as the moment he pulled his t-shirt over her head, he picked her up and laid her on the bed. "Let's see how many calories we can burn, shall we?"

They made love, his lips kissing her body, his fingers caressing her skin as she caressed his. It was slow and gentle and by the time she arched against him and came, she felt the act was an affirmation of the words he'd spoken earlier. He caused her to wonder if she was turning into some sort of sex fiend as her newly laundered panties instantly dampened when he pulled the pumpkin colored dress over her head, smacking his lips the entire time as if remembering how he'd relished the taste of what he was covering with fabric.

They were crawling through the traffic once back in the city.

"It's a good thing you live in Virginia. I can't imagine having to commute every day. What time does your class start tomorrow?"

"Nine but I'm usually there an hour or so earlier. I like to check on the dogs before they start the day."

"So, that's eight. Judging by all these cars, I'll need to get to bed early so I can beat the traffic. How long does it take to get to Quantico? I want to meet the dogs... oh, if that's all right with you?"

Dillon chuckled. "It's not only all right, I was counting on it, but you won't be driving."

"Why not? Is there a commuter train or something that's faster?"

"Babe, if you think I'm letting you out of my sight, you've got another thing coming. You're going to pack some clothes and come back to the farm with me. Unless you'd rather not? In that case, we can bunk in with Owen..."

Charlie smiled. He hadn't said 'he' could bunk with Owen; he'd said 'we'. For that matter, she knew that Martha wouldn't object if they bunked at her house. But, she had to admit, she'd loved being at the farm with him, sharing his house and his bed. She snuggled closer. "No, that's not necessary. I just didn't want to assume you meant to have me as your houseguest."

He slid his hand beneath her skirt, his fingers caressing her thigh. "Houseguest? Is that how you think I see you? If it is, then I obviously need to up my game."

Charlie moaned as his fingers moved again, this time stroking along the gusset of the panties she finally was allowed to put on. "Sir, if you step up your game, I'm going to be nothing but a pool of goo at your feet."

She moaned as his fingertip slipped into her panties to find her slit and slide inside. Her hips shifted, attempting to have it sink further and groaned when instead, it disappeared as a horn honked behind them. She watched as Dillon put his finger into his mouth, giving a moan that had her clit pulse.

"In case you haven't figured it out by now, I am a huge fan of goo."

She shook her head, another dribble joining in that already accumulated to soak her underwear. "You're so bad, MacAllister."

"Only because you are so good, Fullerton."

Once they arrived at Martha's, she collected the key from Mrs. Evans, not wanting to have to worry about it later. The elderly woman was very sweet, but as Martha had warned, wanted to know all about 'Martha's little friend' though, if truth be told, by the way she kept eyeing Dillon, Charlie knew she'd much prefer to talk about her big friend. Dillon was a gentleman, complimenting Mrs. Evans on her home and allowing her to ramble on about her relatives in Dallas for a few minutes before looking at his watch. His statement that he'd love to stay and chat, but unfortunately, they had early dinner reservations, allowed them to slip away graciously.

Martha greeted them with a huge grin and then hugged them both. "I was about to open the door and pretend I had an emergency or something. Owen is on his way here."

Leaving her to chat with Dillon, and praying her friend didn't see fit to offer him further instructions involving her, Charlie ran upstairs and shoved clothes she'd just unpacked a few days earlier back into her duffle. She heard the doorbell ring and then Owen's voice. She stuffed her laptop into its bag and was about to grab all her stuff when Martha walked into the room.

"You're planning on changing, right?"

"Um, not really," Charlie said, looking down at the pumpkin dress she'd worn the night before. "All I've got are jeans and Dillon seems to like this dress—"

"Girl, love must be blind because you obviously didn't give me a second glance."

Charlie saw that her friend was indeed dressed to the nines. She wore a blue silk blouse and a black leather skirt that fit her like a glove. With her black stockings and heels, she looked good enough to be on the menu of any restaurant in the city.

"Put on the black dress," Martha said, going to the closet.

"Dillon didn't dress up so I figured we were going somewhere casual for dinner."

"You figured wrong. Owen brought him some clothes and besides, you can't wear the same thing. We're going to the club after dinner."

Charlie felt her body quiver and yet said that Dillon had to work the following day.

"So do I, but what are we—ninety? Working is not going to keep me home. We don't have to stay late but I wanted to introduce you to Jaxson, Chase, and Emma. Besides, once Dillon sees you in this, he's going to want to show you off, too."

Charlie felt her cheeks heat with pleasure at being someone Dillon would be proud to show off. "I don't know. He said he prefers me in t-shirts."

"Seriously?"

"Well, he does live on a farm—"

"And actually prefers you wearing nothing at all."

Charlie whirled around to see Dillon leaning against the door frame, his arms crossed casually across his chest, a grin on his face.

"You really shouldn't sneak up on a girl," Charlie said.

He just chuckled and nodded towards the dress that still hung on the hanger Martha was holding. "Like I said, naked is better, but I'd love to help you get into that."

Martha smiled, walked to hand him the hanger, and left without another word.

While she changed into the black dress, Dillon changed into a suit.

"You are one gorgeous woman," Dillon said as she stood before him in the black dress and red heels. "I loved the pumpkin dress but might I just say *wow!*"

"Why thank you. And might I say that you are one incredibly handsome man, Sir," she said, picking up her brush only to have Dillon take it from her hand and turn her to face the mirror above the dresser as he began to brush her hair. She moaned. "Why is it so much better when someone else is brushing your hair?"

"Because you're allowing someone to pamper you," Dillon replied, drawing the bristles through her tresses. He bent to kiss the streak of color and then set the brush aside and pulled her back against him. "Get used to it because as much as I'm a fan of goo, I'm also a fan of pampering my girl." He bent to kiss her neck, his hand slipping into the bodice of her dress to cup a breast, rolling her nipple between his fingers until she felt her knees begin to shake.

"If you don't stop that, I'm going to have to change my panties again."

"Again?" His grin had her assured she'd need to do exactly that. God, he could turn her on and off like a faucet with just one look. "I'm also a huge fan of matching lingerie," he said, his eyes meeting hers in the reflection of the mirror.

"I'm not wearing a b..." She stopped speaking when he grinned and she blushed.

"Exactly. Take off your panties and hand them to me, Charlie."

She felt a delicious shiver course through her at the order. It was such a naughty thing to do and yet she only hesitated for a moment. This man was teaching her to be a huge fan of naughty. Slipping the panties off, she handed them to him, praying he really did like pink because her face heated as he put them to his nose and inhaled deeply before tucking them into his jacket pocket.

He carried her suitcase and duffle downstairs and lifted her laptop bag off her shoulder and handed it to Owen. The men went to put in the truck. "I feel like I'm abandoning you," Charlie said as Martha collected her purse in preparation of leaving.

"Are you kidding? This is the happiest I've seen you in years.

Besides, I got to help coax the butterfly out of her cocoon. I couldn't be happier to see that Dillon is now showing that butterfly how it feels to fly."

"I love you, Martha."

"I love you, too, Charlie." Martha gave her a hug and they watched as Dillon began to walk up the sidewalk towards them. "And, I love the fact that the big bad DEA agent is standing next to me with no panties on."

"Martha!" Charlie hissed. "How could you possibly know that! Oh my God, is the back of my dress wet?"

Martha giggled and slipped an arm around Charlie's waist to give her a hug. "No, but you've got this 'I feel naughty' look and Dillon's got this 'I love a naughty girl' look on his face so it was a good guess."

"You are as bad as Dillon," Charlie said, shaking her head.

"God, I should hope so," Martha said with a giggle. "What's the fun in being good all the time?"

CHAPTER 9

"*I*'m driving," Owen said once Martha had locked the door and they all walked down the sidewalk.

"Oh, Dillon said you have a restored Ford," Charlie said, her head swiveling to look up and down the street.

Owen chuckled and beeped a button on his key fob. Lights flashed on a silver Mercedes at the curb. "I do, but I keep it to drive out in the country. Traffic around here can be brutal."

Dillon opened the back door and moved aside to let Charlie climb into the seat. He waited until she was bending to sit before leaning close. "For the rest of the night, you'll lift your dress up and sit on your bare ass." Her face turned red and her eyes flicked to the front where Martha was climbing into the car. "Eyes on me," Dillon said, and was pleased when she instantly returned her gaze to him. "Skirt up, bare ass on the seat."

"Oh... okay," she said, moving her hands behind her to lift her skirt just enough to obey, looking up again when he reached out to stop her.

"Oh, okay?" he asked, arching his eyebrow.

"Um, I meant yes, Sir." He removed his hand from her arm, giving her a smile and a nod. He had to bite back a grin when she gave a little gasp as her bare skin connected with the leather seat and she mumbled, "Guess you've read *The Story of O*, huh?" She swung her legs into the car, the fact that she was sitting as stiff as a statue letting him know that his Charlie had a great deal of new things to experience.

Leaning in, he cupped her chin and then kissed her. "Good girl." Closing her door, he walked around and once he climbed in, he patted the space beside him. "Scoot over here." She didn't exactly scoot but she did lift herself and move the foot required, gasping again when he patted her ass before she could sit. Once she was settled, he draped an arm around her, pulling her into him. He loved the fact that she was so eager to please and yet also loved knowing that his requests could keep her off balance. "No, but I'm thoroughly enjoying writing *The Story of C.*"

She groaned, but smiled when he bent to kiss the top of her head, relaxing against him with the simple gesture.

As Owen maneuvered through traffic, Martha pointed out various landmarks. Dillon waited for a break in the verbal tour to ask Charlie, "You've never been to D.C. before?"

"No. After college, Martha moved back to D.C. as she's from here but I'm a native Texan. I accepted a job and did my training there as well. I suppose I should be at least a little guilty that I've not yet done the entire touristy thing."

"Ah, I remember you saying something about not being a huge fan of cold marble men," Dillon said, sliding his hand down her bare arm. "Let's see, what was it exactly? Oh yes, you said you'd much rather ride a hot blooded FBI agent."

"I did not!" Charlie said. "I was talking about riding with you... I mean horseback riding!" Martha giggled from the front seat and Charlie shook her head. "You're impossible, you know."

"You're adorable," he said, bending to kiss her cheek. "But it really is a shame that you haven't seen the memorials."

"I'd much rather look at fields and play with the puppies." She lifted her head from his shoulder and said, "And, of course, play with you."

He kissed her lightly and dropped his arm, sliding his hand beneath her naked buttock, giving it a squeeze. "I'm very glad because I am thinking of all sorts of delightful games we can play."

Owen pulled the car under the awning in front of the restaurant. A valet stepped forward and opened the doors. Dillon slid his hand from its hiding place and stepped out, turning to offer Charlie his hand. She hesitated, as if judging the best way to slide across the seat and he grinned. It was delightful watching her inner submissive struggle with the 'good girl' image that had probably been drilled in her since birth. Finally, she took his hand and allowed him to help her slide across the seat. He didn't miss her look back and knew she feared she'd left a puddle on the leather. Bending down, he whispered, "Don't forget, you're in the company of fellow kinksters. A little wet spot is to be expected."

"Oh my God," she moaned, and sure enough, the color he'd come to crave appeared on her cheeks.

Owen had chosen well, the restaurant was quiet and elegant. They were led to a table in front of a bank of windows, the dome of the capital building as their backdrop. Dillon pulled out a chair and as Charlie began to sit, he whispered, "Dress up."

"Here?"

"Everywhere tonight," he confirmed.

She darted her eyes about but must have decided that she'd draw more attention to herself half crouched than seated, so with a lift of her hands, her skirt came up and she sat. Dillon pushed in her chair, bent to kiss her cheek and took his own seat. "What would you like to drink?" he asked.

"A glass of chardonnay, please," she said and Martha decided to have one as well. Their drinks arrived and Dillon lifted his glass.

"A toast. Thank you Martha for being Charlie's friend and for bringing her back into my life."

Martha smiled. "And thank you for not letting the butterfly

slip back into her cocoon." They all clinked their glasses. They talked for a few minutes and then opened their menus.

"Don't order just a salad," Dillon said. "You're going to need your energy."

Charlie looked at him and smiled. "In that case, what would you suggest? I'm more of a BBQ or Tex-Mex kind of gal."

"You have any allergies?" he asked and when she said she didn't, he suggested she have the surf and turf.

"I'll have the surf," she countered. "Eating too much causes me to get sleepy. I'd hate to fall asleep on you."

He chuckled and they placed their orders. While they waited, Martha asked about the farm and Dillon enjoyed listening to Charlie's excitement as she talked about the dogs. "They are so cute and so amazingly smart. I can't wait to watch Dillon tomorrow."

"Charlie told me that Lucy is a German Shepherd. Is that the only breed used in the K-9 corps?" Martha asked.

Dillon shook his head. "No, when the corps started there were over thirty breeds originally approved for training. However, it didn't take long before that was changed. There are seven breeds used now. I've worked with huskies and collies, but German Shepherds are what I see most."

They talked about the training a bit and he smiled. "I've found that a lot of the times, it's not the dogs that require the most training; it's their partners. You've got to be in good physical condition as well. But the most vital thing is to match the right person with the right dog. You make that connection and there is nothing better than watching that bond grow so strong."

"Well, I can't wait to watch," Charlie said, taking a roll from the basket on the table.

Owen chuckled. "Just be prepared. If I know my little brother, and I do, he'll have you running the course with the others. Speaking from experience, it can be pretty brutal. You'll be climbing walls, swinging from ropes, and crawling through mud."

"Really? Oh, wow, that sounds fantastic!"

Martha shook her head. "And here you complained about that facial mask at the spa."

Charlie laughed and shrugged. "True, but this sounds like fun!"

Their food arrived and when Charlie's enthusiasm dimmed, Dillon looked over. "What's the matter?"

"I- I didn't expect it to look like that," she said, pointing to her plate. "It's staring at me!"

Dillon chuckled and reached for her plate where an entire lobster was presented on a bed of rice pilaf. He expertly cracked open the lobster shell, reducing it to edible segments and tucking the head, and eyes, away on his plate before setting the meal back in front of Charlie.

"Thank you," she said, "I expected just the tail."

"Like I said, you're going to need your energy and I'm not talking about the obstacle course tomorrow. You'll need a big breakfast as well."

Charlie dipped her first bite into the melted butter and put it into her mouth, giving that moan that he so loved to hear. This woman was not only intelligent and gorgeous, she had an enthusiasm and love of life that was absolutely charming. He couldn't wait to put her through her paces... both at Black Light and Quantico, not doubting for a moment that she'd excel in both.

Each couple agreed to split a dessert. Owen and Martha picked a seven-layer slice of chocolate cake with a decadent layer of chocolate ganache between each layer. Dillon and Charlie chose a slice of cheesecake covered with a raspberry puree and dotted with fresh berries.

"This is positively sinful," Charlie exclaimed as she took a bite of the cheesecake.

"I agree," Dillon said, taking his own bite and then leaning towards her, another bite on his fork. "It's a sin to have to settle for these berries when what I really want are to nibble on yours."

She turned as red as the raspberries as she accepted the bite. "You're incorrigible," she said once she'd swallowed.

"Baby, you haven't even begun to see what incorrigible looks like," he countered, his eyes locked on hers. "But you will." He paid the check and stood, offering Charlie his hand. Pulling her up, he leaned down and kissed her. "Ready to play?"

"Very ready," she said, her eyes sparkling.

When they entered the psychic shop, the woman was again seated at the table. She smiled and nodded, tilting her head towards the curtain. Luis opened the door and the four of them walked through.

"This is just so cool," Charlie said as they walked down the tunnel. "It's unlike any other club I've been in. Frankly, I'm a little surprised there's no secret handshake."

"Well, there kind of is," Martha said. "You didn't get to see it last night because I'm not a full member, but… Dillon are you a member or come as a guest occasionally?"

"Are you kidding? I couldn't sign up fast enough once Owen told me about the club's existence."

"Good, then you can demonstrate the secret handshake for Charlie. Oh, and are you still going by Rose?"

"I'm not sure I understand the need for using a different name. I mean, I saw a lot of faces last night that I've seen in the newspaper or on TV and understand that they might want to, but Owen and Dillon don't use aliases."

Martha giggled. "Leave it up to you to consider it as an alias versus a pseudonym."

"If I left it up to you, I'd be called Tex," Charlie shot back.

Dillon chuckled. "You are definitely not someone who looks like a Tex. But, it's totally up to you. You're both my Charlie and my yellow Rose, so your choice." He grinned. "Or, you can do what a lot of guests do and pick something that describes you instead of a name. Some submissives choose things like 'Daddy's Girl' or 'Princess'."

"Um, no thanks. I'll stick with Charlie if that's all right."

"Then Charlie it is," Dillon said as they approached the desk where Danny was sitting.

"Welcome back," Danny said with a smile.

"Okay, Charlie, pay attention and watch this," Martha said, "Go ahead, Dillon, show her."

"Good grief, Marty, are you ever going to stop topping from the bottom?" Owen asked.

"Hmmm, perhaps I need some private lessons," she said, fluttering her lashes up at him. "Perhaps you can recommend someone, Sir?"

"Maybe we should start calling you Brat," Owen said, but was smiling as he did.

Dillon pulled Charlie closer and then flipped his palm up, passing his wrist under a light. Where there had been nothing before, his skin now glowed, showing the two letters, BL, and some kind of bar code beneath that.

"Oh, wow, that's even better than a secret handshake," Charlie said, watching the tattoo disappear once Dillon pulled his hand free.

"Keeps members from having to carry their wallets," Dillon explained. "Everything from drinks, food, and toys are put on your account with a single scan." He led her to the frosted window and demonstrated again as he paid for a guest pass. Once Martha had signed in, they placed their purses with their phones inside a locker, Dillon adding his wallet, keys, phone, and watch.

The club was packed even though it was a Sunday night. Owen left them to go change for duty, but the trio went to the bar. Dillon sat on a stool and then lifted Charlie onto his lap, causing her to blush as he swept her skirt back before setting her down. "What would you like to drink? There's a two drink limit and since we had wine at dinner, you're allowed one more."

"Really? That seems a bit unusual as liquor is normally where a club makes most of its money."

127

"It's actually a good policy. This isn't a normal club and making safe, sane, and consensual choices is easier if you're not blitzed," Dillon explained.

Charlie ordered a vodka and cranberry and Martha requested a screwdriver. Once their drinks and Dillon's bourbon arrived, his tattoo was scanned to pay. They had just taken their first sips when another trio approached them.

"Charlie, let me introduce you to the brilliant people who opened the two hottest clubs in town," Dillon said. "This is Jaxson Davidson, Chase Cartwright, and this lovely lady, is Emma Fischer. This is Charlie."

"It's a pleasure to meet you, Charlie," Jaxson said, shaking her hand. "We saw you last night but never got a chance to come over and introduce ourselves."

"Wow, you both look even better in person than in all those magazine spreads." Charlie said, her eyes wide and her cheeks pinkening. "Well, that sounded a bit stalkerish. I meant to say, both your clubs are incredible."

"I knew I was going to like you," Chase said, foregoing the handshake, lifting her hand and kissing the back of it instead.

"And, at the risk of sounding even more like an idiot, I want to say what you three did... that night of the senator's fundraiser, being totally open about your relationship, well, that was even more incredible than this club."

"You don't sound like an idiot at all. I know it had to shock a great deal of people, but it was actually very freeing. I hope to get to know you a lot better," Emma said, reaching over and giving Charlie a hug.

"I'd like that," Charlie said.

They chatted for a few more minutes and then left to speak to other members. "It's nice to see they are really as happy as they appear in photographs," Charlie said as they watched them walk away, Emma between the two men who both had arms wrapped around her back.

"Yes, it's even better that they opened a fabulous place where others can enjoy their kink," Marty said. "And speaking of kink, it's time for me to find a partner."

"Oh, I thought maybe you and Owen—" Charlie began.

"Keep sending those positive vibes," Marty said, jumping off her stool. "I figure that sooner or later that man won't be able to resist giving me a lesson or two. I'll catch up with you in a bit."

"Owen's not going to know what hit him," Charlie said. "When Marty sets her mind on a goal, she doesn't stop until she reaches it."

Dillon grinned. "Don't underestimate my brother. He's just enjoying playing cat and mouse." He took the last swallow of his drink and set it down. "You didn't get to see much of the club last night. How about I give you a tour?"

"Sounds good," Charlie said, finishing her drink as well.

Plucking her from the stool, Dillon placed his hand at the small of her back, his fingers caressing bare skin. He bent and kissed her cheek. "I am a huge fan of this dress." He waited until she looked up and smiled before he added, "But, it is still coming off."

With her blushing again, he began the tour. "As you saw last night, there are some raised platforms. They can be rearranged as needed but are generally used for demonstrations." He pointed towards one side of the room. "Those booths are available for semi-private play. Some have small beds, one a chaise lounge, and another has a massage table. The curtains can be closed if more privacy is desired."

He pointed out a coed bathroom, explaining that there were showers inside that were available and often shared. When she asked if there were separate restrooms, he pointed those out as well, explaining there were cubbyholes inside where clothing could be left if desired. As they walked, they passed people who were simply chatting but joined a group who were watching a scene. A woman had been bound to the St. Andrew's cross and two men were wielding floggers against her back and ass. Several spectators were seated on loveseats in a semi-circle and others stood. Dillon didn't watch the trio, he watched Charlie. She was so focused on the scene that when he slipped behind her and slid his hand into her bodice to play with her breasts, she startled and then leaned against him. Her nipples were already hard little points. They watched until the woman arched and screamed, her body convulsing as she came. The men untied her, positioning her on her hands and knees to take their own pleasure, but Dillon had a different agenda.

"Are you ready to begin our game?" he asked, kissing the nape of her neck, loving the tiny purr she gave.

"Yes, Sir, but you haven't told me what game we are playing."

"You'll see, but first, we need to do a little shopping."

She looked up at him, her nose crinkled. "We're going shopping? We just got here."

"This is not only a great club, its owners are savvy enough to know that where there are games to be played, there are toys to be bought. As Sherlock Holmes said, 'Let the games begin.'"

CHAPTER 10

*C*harlie watched with a mixture of excitement and trepidation as she studied various items on display in the glass cabinets of the 'store'. She saw different types of lubes next to shelves with dildos of every size and color as well as shorter, fatter plugs that made her bottom clench with the memory of Dillon inserting such a toy in her ass. The sight of shiny silver clamps made Charlie's nipples pucker at the thought of having the sensitive little buds caught in the clamp's wicked little teeth. The variety of implements amazed her. Everything from paddles made of wood, plastic, or leather, as well as crops were waiting to set a submissive's ass on fire. She felt her breath catch at the display of floggers, the falls spread out in a fan pattern so that a prospective buyer could make their choice of smooth strands or knotted ones as well as choose which type of material they preferred. Her mind was whirling with all the infinite, delicious possibilities when the woman behind the counter turned to them.

"Good evening, Sir, may I help you?"

"Good evening. Yes, I believe you have an order ready for me, Dillon MacAllister?"

"Yes, Sir. Just a moment."

As she stepped away, Dillon turned to look down at Charlie who was shaking her head. "What? You didn't think I was going to spoil the surprise did you? What sort of game would it be if I left clues right out in the open?"

Though she really had hoped to see what he'd choose, Charlie had to admit that allowing her to peruse all the offerings and yet not know what he'd decided upon added to the anticipation. She smiled up at him. "I do love solving a good mystery, Mr. Holmes."

"That's the spirit. Shall we make it a bit more difficult, my beautiful Watson?" Dillon pulled her to him and moved her a few feet down the counter. "Pick one," he instructed, waving his hand over the glass behind which various blindfolds were displayed. A shiver ran through Charlie. Not only was he not allowing her to see the toys he'd be using in their play, he was obviously going to be denying her the sense of sight during their scene.

"The red is very pretty," Charlie said.

"It is and you will look stunning wearing nothing but it and your red heels."

Charlie wondered if it were possible to come from anticipation alone, as her body responded to his words.

"Here you are, Mr. MacAllister," the clerk said as she set a bag on the counter.

"And the red blindfold, please."

"A lovely choice." The woman removed the blindfold and when she began to open the bag to put it inside, Dillon stopped her, taking it and turning to Charlie.

"Turn around," he instructed.

Though she hadn't expected to be blindfolded so quickly, she turned and closed her eyes as he placed the blindfold over them, and tied it behind her head. It wasn't unlike just shutting her eyes and yet the psychological effect was immediate. She realized that she'd not be able to take a single step without Dillon to guide her. Already having a submissive nature, she felt a deeper sense of trust given to her Dom. When he turned her again, she felt a bit unsteady on her feet which had nothing to do with the fact she was wearing stilettos.

"Put your hand on my arm. It will help your balance," Dillon instructed, guiding her hand to his forearm and giving it a squeeze.

"Thank you, Mr. MacAllister. Enjoy your evening."

"We shall," Dillon said and then again placed his hand over hers. "We're going to walk slowly but I won't let you go."

"Thank you, Sir," she said. It was strange and yet exciting. She knew they passed people as she could hear voices coming and going. The club was crowded and yet, true to his word, she never even brushed against another person.

With her sight gone, every other sense she possessed seemed heightened. When Dillon paused a few moments before stepping forward again, she felt the sound of the club dimming. Even the air felt different, cooler somehow. The click of her heels changed, each step was louder and there was a brief echo heard before the next click. Where were they? Had he taken her into one of those booths he'd pointed out? As she took a few more steps, she didn't believe so as those were not as spacious as the floor they were crossing. It was another few moments before he halted again.

Her hand was lifted from his arm and guided in front of her. "Hold onto the edge of the table," he instructed. She did so with both hands, her fingers encountering not the padded leather she expected but solid unyielding wood. From the span her hands had to open to grip the edge, she knew it was thick wood, and from the stroke of her fingertips, it was smooth as glass. For some reason, she envisioned a beautifully handcrafted table from eons past.

All thoughts of the table's appearance disappeared when she felt Dillon behind her, the sound of the zipper of her dress being lowered, the sensation of his fingertips sliding the straps from her shoulders. She couldn't stop the shiver that ran through her as the fabric slid from her skin, exposing her to him, to the room.

"Step out," he instructed and once she did, she was exactly as he'd described. Completely nude but for the red blindfold and the matching heels on her feet. Warmth enveloped her as Dillon pressed against her back, his hands snaking around her waist.

"Tonight is about sensation," he explained, speaking softly. "Touch is a sense that we take for granted, one we don't really consider. Tonight that will change. It can be gentle and soft…" He paused and she gasped as her breasts were taken, his fingers stroking lightly across her flesh. "It can be harsh." She jerked as fingers took her nipples and squeezed.

"Touch can bring pleasure or pain, or a combination of both," he continued, releasing her nipples to soothe them with gentle, circling motions. "I want you to relax, don't think, just feel. Allow your body to experience every sensation, every touch. You remember the safe words, correct?"

"Yes, Sir." God, why did her heart leap with that question?

"Relax, Charlie. This is also about trust. Trust that as your Dom, my goal is to make this an experience that will not only test your limits, but one you'll enjoy." She shivered again as he lifted the weight of her hair then pressed his lips against the nape of her neck. It was another lesson in sensation as she felt the wetness of his tongue licking a path from her collarbone, up the side of her neck to the spot behind her ear. Warmth followed as he blew along the trail, her nipples crinkling and her pussy dampening as he suckled the lobe of her ear, drawing on it and then, without warning, biting down, and at the same time, pinching her nipples tightly again.

"Ahhh," she moaned, her body shuddering.

He released her to say, "I'm going to lift you onto the table. Place your arms above your head and spread your legs wide." Not waiting for her to respond, he lifted her and then laid her upon the surface. Charlie discovered that the hard surface she expected wasn't what she felt. Instead of wood, she felt a softness that indicated he'd laid her on some sort of padded surface and felt the leather cushion her body. Remembering his instructions, she lifted her arms and spread her legs.

A new sensation flowed through her as she felt him putting her wrists into padded cuffs, hearing a click as he joined them together, guiding her fingers around some sort of bar. Her ankles were next, both cuffed and secured to the table. Splayed open, her body his to do with as he wished, sent her deeper into submission. She startled and then moaned as his mouth descended on hers, the kiss so soft and then demanding as he pushed his tongue between her lips to possess her. Without sight to look into his eyes, to see his expression heightened the kiss. It was as intoxicating as anything she'd ever experienced.

He pulled away and her tongue came out to lick along her lips, already wishing his would return. Her head tilted to the side, trying to determine where he was but instead heard the sound of him opening the bag that she'd forgotten he'd even had. What was hidden inside? What toy or implement would she experience without seeing? He was right… this was a game of mystery and suspense. A game in which the only rule she'd been given was to relax, to feel, to accept whatever sensation her dominant chose to gift her with.

Her body jerked again when something trailed between her breasts to her pubis. "Relax, Charlie, don't use your mind to figure out what it is; let your senses be the detective."

It was hard to obey. Not that she didn't trust him, but she was a woman who was constantly observing. Her very job depended on her ability to quickly assess her surroundings, to eliminate areas of danger that threatened her very safety. The object reversed its path, to circle the mounds of her breasts, the flutter over her nipples that seemed to make up their own mind that they enjoyed the touch as they pebbled even tighter. Listening to her body instead of her mind, she relaxed into the table, unclenching fingers that had held the bar so tightly. She squirmed a bit when the sensation moved to her armpit and then snaked down her side.

"Ticklish?" he asked, amusement in his tone.

"No... just surprised." Her denial proved to be a lie as he switched sides and she jerked in the other direction when the sensation turned from soft to sharp before going soft again.

"Definitely ticklish," Dillon said, continuing to stroke all over her body, to tease, to torment until she was breathless. "You look so sweet, squirming about, your body covered with thousands of goose bumps." He bent to kiss her again, her body arching in need that was briefly provided before he pulled away again.

The next sensation was one that had her gasp as warmth flowed down her body. He'd poured something into the valley between her breasts and then trickled it down her stomach and then dribbled along each of her legs. Though there was no scent, its very viscosity told Charlie he'd used some type of oil. She shuddered as she felt some drip from her pubis to run along her sex and then the crack of her ass but when strong fingers began to spread the oil, she moaned with pleasure. Dillon began at her calves, massaging the oil into her skin, the warmth spreading as muscles relaxed and the oil heated beneath his palms. Her legs quivered as he moved up them slowly, her thighs trembling as he stroked the oil over every inch before massaging each one. She arched her hips up, silently asking that he not forget her sex where her own moisture was adding to the slickness between her legs, and yet when he obeyed her unspoken request, she moaned in frustration as it was only the briefest of touches before his hand moved to continue to distribute the oil across her abdomen.

"Oh, God," she whispered as fingers, now slickened by the oil began to roll and pull on her nipples, plucking and releasing, tugging and twisting until her back arched with the pleasure and pain combination he'd spoken of earlier. The massage continued to include each breast, fingers rubbing the oil until each one was coated, every inch explored. When his hands reached her shoulders, she again arched. "Please... please, Sir..." not knowing what she was asking for, just knowing that she needed more.

Dillon's response was to kiss her once more as he finished the massage, only to step away. Charlie could imagine what she must look like. Her naked body would be glistening, her nipples tight, her pussy slick.

"Oh, yes, thank you, Sir," she said as she felt his fingers returning to her pussy, spreading labia lips that she knew must be swollen, plump with the blood that was drawn to the area with her arousal. She thrust her hips up as she felt his lips draw her clit inside, the coil that had begun to wind inside her from the moment he'd tied the blindfold going tighter. She keened with pleasure and them mewed with distress as his lips released her after giving her clit a bite.

Fingers slid between her lips, stroking each fold, pressing them apart. She blushed, imagining them opening like the petals of a flower... like a rose. When a finger slid inside, she groaned, once again pulling on the bar above her head, her feet flexing with pleasure as a second finger joined the first. She forgot to think as the sensations overtook her, each push forward stretching her, each withdrawal leaving her empty for the briefest moment.

When she thought she understood the rhythm, the dance changed. Something cold pressed against her entrance had her gasping, stiffening. As Dillon began to press it inside, she groaned as the object stretched her further than his fingers, filled her more completely. The shock of the coldness dissipated as her body warmed the object. At first she thought it was a dildo and yet, when Dillon pushed it further inside her and then removed his fingers, she realized it wasn't. Trying to determine what it was instantly stopped as she felt another object pressing inside. This one felt heavier somehow but just as he had the first, he pressed it up inside her until it settled against the first.

His lips descended on her clit again and as he suckled, her pussy spasmed and she felt her muscles clench around the objects.

Again and again, she spasmed and the items moved, rolled and she suddenly remembered his promise of earlier. She had no doubt that he'd pressed some type of balls inside her. Satisfied that she'd uncovered the identity of one of the mystery objects, she was totally unprepared when a sudden jolt had her gasping loudly.

"Oh my God!" she moaned as the balls began to vibrate inside her, seeming to increase in size as the vibrations stimulated the very sensitive walls of her cunt. She had barely absorbed the fact that he was using some kind of remote when she gasped again at the feeling of something pressing against her anus. Her whimper was ignored as the object began to push inside, and though it stretched her muscle, it didn't seem very large and she could tell it was slick as the rest of her body.

"Relax, Charlie, this is but the first," Dillon said, pressing a bit harder until she gave a small gasp as the object defeated her muscle to slip inside. Her relief was short lived as a second ball was inserted, and then a third, each one forcing her sphincter to open a bit wider to accept the spheres which were increasing in size.

"Oh... oh, God," she moaned. "I don't... too much..."

"Color?" Dillon asked, pausing with the insertion of the fourth.

Charlie didn't immediately respond and then whispered, "Green... but... yes, green, Sir."

"Good girl," Dillon praised and she felt his lips kiss her inner thigh. "Just a few more."

A few more? How many were a few? There was no need to voice the questions as she would discover the answer as he continued. A fifth ball joined the others, then another and another until she couldn't believe her body had actually accepted nine of the slick orbs into a place she'd only had invaded with his finger and a butt plug.

"Last one."

"Oh... oh, Dill... Sir," she moaned, positive she couldn't hold another. "Oh, God!" she yelled, not with the tenth ball's insertion but from the sudden, powerful vibrations of the balls he'd inserted into her pussy. She continued to moan, her body coiling as the pressure on her back passage increased until with a final cry, the last ball slid inside.

"Beautiful," Dillon said, his kiss of what she was sure was now her widely stretched anus, adding to the heat that suffused her entire body as the coil tightened until it threatened to break.

"No!" she whined when, with a click of the remote, the vibrations inside her went from pulsing to barely felt. "Oh, please... please... I need to come."

Dillon kissed the lips between her legs, kissed her throbbing clit before moving up her body, dropping kisses over slickened skin, nipping the ripe berries of her nipples before once more taking her mouth.

"There is nothing more beautiful than you at this moment," he said, pulling away, his hand stroking her hair off her forehead. "So wanting, so pliant, so accepting. But, my love, we are not yet done."

Charlie didn't know what to expect and realized that was the purpose of the game. With both her pussy and ass full, she felt sensations she'd never imagined. Every time her muscles clenched, they contracted around the balls he'd filled her with. She felt both heavy and light at the same time and couldn't fathom how that could be possible. When the next sensation came, it had her arching her back. It was hot... no cold. Sharp... wait, no it was a dull pressure. Whatever it was, it was moving around her right breast in a spiral pattern. Her pussy and ass clenched as she realized that with every rotation, it was nearing her poor defenseless nipple.

"Ahhhhhhh!" she squealed as the object rolled across her taut point. And though she briefly wondered if she was feeling the bite of a nipple clamp, the sensation dissipated when the object moved down the slope of her right breast, leaving a tingling trail across the valley before beginning to circle her left breast. She moaned, she gasped, she shuddered... she did everything but think. When the path was changed to roll down her belly, she whimpered, she bit her lip, she moaned and when it rolled across her tender labia lips, she surrendered. Every cell of her body absorbed the sensations: warm lips kissing her skin as Dillon kissed her body; sharp pricks of pain as the object was rolled over the sensitive skin of her underarms; her clit throbbed as the object moved to circle it again and again; nerve endings pulsing; synapses snapping as the vibrations in her pussy began again only to have her body arch as every ball in her ass began to vibrate as well, a pulsating beat that had her sure that if she didn't find release, she'd die.

Her mouth opened in a silent scream of ecstasy, stars burst beneath her eyelids as with a single pull, the balls were pulled from her ass and she exploded. The scream became audible, reverberating off the walls as with one thrust, Dillon's cock took the place of the anal balls. Warmth pressed down on her as he laid his body over hers. Her world was nothing but sensation; no thoughts existed as she came again, fluid gushing from her pussy as his cock pistoned in and out of her ass. She wasn't aware that her restraints had been undone until she found her arms clinging to him, her legs wrapped around his waist, pulling him closer as he fucked her, filled her, claimed her last virgin passage. Spiraling up again, unable to stop the ascent, she could do nothing but accept the demand of her very soul that she splinter yet again and it took her a moment to realize that the blindfold was gone as her vision was filled with molten chocolate eyes as Dillon joined her in bliss.

Thunderous applause from spectators had Charlie blushing, realizing for the first time that they hadn't been alone. She closed her eyes only to hear Dillon whispering that the crowd was showing their appreciation for such a beautiful scene. "I'm so very proud of you, baby."

She felt completely boneless as Dillon swept her off the table, carrying her a few steps before he sank onto a loveseat, holding her close. Nerves kept snapping, her body trembling as he caressed her, massaging her arms, her back, fingers stroking through her hair. She was only capable of giving the softest mews as she came down from the most mind-blowing sex she'd ever had. Every inch of her skin felt hypersensitive, her pussy continuing to pulse as she snuggled into his body. It was several minutes before she could even begin to put thoughts together and a few more before she could speak.

"That... that was..."

"Sensational?" Dillon offered with a grin.

Charlie smiled and nodded. It was the perfect word after all. She accepted a bottle of juice, drinking it slowly until it was gone, only to be given another one.

"Drink it all, baby. You expended a lot more energy than you'd believe."

She obeyed, allowing the liquid to replenish her. Once it was mostly gone, she smiled, running a fingertip down his chest. "You're as oily as I am."

Dillon chuckled. "And here I thought your first real sentence would be a question as to what was used on your gorgeous body."

Charlie laughed. "I tried to guess for a while but then... just felt. It doesn't really matter what the game pieces were, it was the most incredible, amazing game I've ever played."

"I'm glad you enjoyed it," Dillon said, bending to kiss her gently. "Then I suppose I can just tuck them back into the bag and..."

"No! I mean, please, Sir, I'd like to see."

"Care to guess first?"

Charlie nestled closer, remembering back to the start of their play. "I thought at first you used a feather but though it was soft, sometimes it felt prickly."

"That was because it was a feather quill," Dillon said.

"Ah, that makes sense. Okay, I know you used some type of

oil… and might I add that you, Sir, can give me a massage any day. You have the most sensual, strong hands. It was fantastic."

"Good to know. And the next?"

Charlie blushed. "At first I thought it was a dildo like the ones in the shop, but it was too small and when you added another, I remembered when you said playing with balls would be in my future." She smiled and shook her head. "I'm guessing now you didn't mean tennis balls."

Dillon chuckled. "No, these were ben wa balls."

"So you put several up my ass as well?"

He shook his head. "No, that was a string of anal beads. And might I add, you handled them extremely well."

"To be honest, I thought I'd split open when you first started but… well, they were pretty amazing. God, when everything started vibrating, I thought I was going to die. Oh, what was the other thing? I couldn't decide if it was hot or cold and it felt both sharp and dull." She shuddered remembering the item traveling all over her flesh.

"That was a Wartenberg wheel. Doctors use them to test for nerve function." He paused and ran a hand down her arm. "Doms use it to drive their subs wild."

"Well, it worked. I felt as if every nerve in my body was on fire."

Dillon kissed her again and when he released her, he said, "Let's go shower and then get you home." He set her on the loveseat as he gathered the toys he'd used and their clothing.

"We're not… walking out there naked are we?" she asked when it became apparent that he wasn't intending to hand her dress to her.

Dillon laughed again. "Did you forget we are in a sex club?"

Charlie opened her mouth and then closed it. She wasn't about to admit that yes, she'd totally forgotten. Where the club was modern, bright and open, this room—no, this dungeon—was exactly how she imagined ones beneath the floors of ancient castles to be. But though it was small and dim, flickering lights representing flames in sconces along the walls, instead of fear, she felt her insides quickening again. Equipment she could see included a set of stocks, a large St. Andrew's cross, and another raised table.

"Ready?" Dillon's question snapped her back to the present and she took his extended hand. It wasn't until she took a step that she pulled up short.

"Um... Dillon?" she whispered though the room had cleared out.

"Honey, no one is going to care that you're naked—"

"No, it's not that," Charlie began, glad the room was dim as she was positive her face was scarlet. The moment she'd started walking, she'd felt the movements of the balls still tucked up inside her pussy. "What... what if the ben wa balls fall out?"

Dillon's grin had her face heating even more. "Well, that they might notice. So, baby, I suggest you let the need to concentrate on keeping them inside take your mind off the fact that you're nude."

She groaned but did tighten her pelvic muscles as he slipped an arm around her waist. And, as he'd suggested, she barely noticed the people they passed, and didn't care a bit that she was a glistening, naked woman as her Dominant led her across the club.

Charlie discovered that the coed shower room wasn't only for cleaning off. After Dillon set their clothes into a cubby, she blushed as he squatted before her. "Okay, push down."

"Oh, God," she whispered... embarrassed to have to release the ben wa balls out in the open until she realized that other people in the room were not the least bit interested in what she was doing. They were too involved in their own enjoyment to even glance her way. After Dillon had caught the toys, they washed the ben wa balls and anal bead string as well before soaping each other. Dillon dried her with a thick fluffy towel. As he fastened her dress, she could barely keep her eyes open.

"Just a bit longer and then you can curl up and sleep on the way home," Dillon promised, pulling on his clothing and guiding her from the room. They found Owen and as Dillon told him they were heading out; Charlie was aware enough to notice he was scowling a bit. Looking over her shoulder, she saw Marty sitting on the lap of some man, her face animated, obviously telling some sort of story by the way her hands were constantly moving. When Marty looked up and caught her eye, Charlie smiled and gave her a little wave, mouthing, "See you later." Marty nodded, gave a quick glance to the two brothers, and then returned her attention to her companion, draping her arms around his neck. As Dillon led her from the club, Charlie was still smiling. It seemed that Owen might need to step up his game if he had any interest in the feisty accountant.

CHAPTER 11

*D*illon woke her early the next morning with a kiss. When she grumbled, he ran his hand down her side and cupped her bottom cheek. "Up and at 'em, recruit," he said, giving her ass a swat.

"You're a sadist, MacAllister," she said, sitting up in the bed.

"That's Special Agent MacAllister today, young lady. Get dressed and come downstairs... and that means in the next five minutes. Don't you dare go back to sleep."

"Lord, you are bossy."

Dillon laughed and pulled her up, giving her a hug and another kiss. "Get used to it. Today is going to be full of orders for you to obey."

"Hmmm, maybe I'll just stay here and play with the puppies."

"Well, suit yourself, but if you're too chicken to run a real obstacle course instead of those wimpy courses the DEA thinks are badass, then, I suppose—"

"Take that back!" Charlie said, her eyes finally clearing. "I bet I can run your course with one hand tied behind my back."

He grinned and pulled her closer, his hands cupping her bare butt. "As much as I love to see you bound, I'm afraid that would be a safety infraction. Besides, don't you want to eat in the cafeteria?"

Charlie laughed. "Well why didn't you say that in the first place?" He gave her butt a slap and released her. He was at the door before she said, "Wait, what should I wear?"

"Did you pack those sexy little khaki shorts you ran around in down in Brownsville?"

"You've got a strange sense of fashion, Agent MacAllister, but yes."

"Wear them and a t-shirt, socks and tennis shoes. Oh, and pull your hair up. It will make a useful handle if I have to tug you up the wall."

"Very funny. It's going to be a very short handle," she muttered but moved to where her suitcase had been placed. Dillon left her to get ready as he returned to the kitchen.

A few minutes later, he looked up and grinned. "Well, well, how did you know?" he asked.

"Know what?" she asked nonchalantly, but her twitching lips gave her away.

Evidently Charlie had found one of Lucy's rawhide bones as it was now balanced on top of her head, her black ponytail sticking straight up. She looked just like Pebbles of *The Flintstones*. He turned off the burner on the stove and began to stalk towards her, leering as her smile vanished and she started backing away. "It's always been a fantasy of mine to go back in time to visit the stone age... especially as I fell in love with Pebbles years ago and have been blessed with my own club." She whirled and streaked away, the bone sliding off her head as he took off after her. It didn't take long to catch her, popping her butt as he chanted, "Bam... bam, bam."

"I couldn't resist," she squealed, wiggling for all she was worth as Lucy bounced around the couple as if wanting to join the fun.

"You are just too damned cute." He kissed her and retrieved the bone, tossing it to Lucy before leading Charlie back into the kitchen and handing her a mug of coffee.

"I can't possibly eat all this," she complained a moment later when he placed a plate piled high with scrambled eggs, bacon, a thick slice of ham, crisp hash browns and two pieces of toast in front of her.

"You can and you will," Dillon corrected. "You're going to be burning a lot of calories today."

"So that part about the cafeteria was just a lie?" she asked, buttering a piece of toast.

"Nope, you'll need to refuel then before the afternoon session." He joined her at the table, grinning as she rolled her eyes again. He knew she'd be grateful she'd eaten a hearty breakfast by the time lunch rolled around.

Charlie had practically bounced on the seat the entire drive to Quantico. Lucy sat on her other side, seeming as amused as he about Charlie's excitement. He stopped at the gate, signed in, adding her name as a visitor and then drove onto the grounds.

Charlie's head swiveled as she looked out the windows. "How big is Quantico?"

"Pretty big," Dillon said as he made a turn. "There are over 500 acres with several areas serving different purposes. We have the FBI academy here as well as buildings for forensic training, and other administration facilities. There are gun ranges, various obstacle courses, some for humans and then there are ones designed for K-9 training. We've got mock-ups of what one might expect to find in war zones, buildings set up to train dogs to find drugs and others set up to search for survivors or recover bodies after man-made or natural disasters."

She looked up at him, stilling at the thought of disasters. "Do you use real bodies?"

"Yes. Have you ever read any books by Patricia Cromwell?" At her nod, he continued. "Her novel *Body Farm* includes information about forensics and the decay of a human body. It sounds a bit morbid, but the research has improved knowledge from everything about how to determine how long a body has been buried by studying insect activity, to how to judge the cause of death. Without people dedicating their remains to science, forensics wouldn't be as exact a science as it is now."

She nodded her understanding and turned her attention back to the windows as they passed a large group of people running in formation. "This reminds me of my training," Charlie said. "Some days I thought my legs were made of rubber from all the miles we had to run."

"Yes, it's pretty intensive, but I must say, all that running has given you some mighty fine legs, Agent Fullerton." He emphasized his point by running his hand over her bare thigh, slipping his fingers beneath the hem of her shorts.

"Watch it, Agent MacAllister," she said as she pulled at his wrist. "It wouldn't do for the teacher to be seen mauling his student."

"Oh, Charlie, that comment just brought up the sexiest little image of you in a short little plaid skirt, a white blouse, knee socks, and of course, a pair of white little panties just waiting to come down."

"So not fair," she said as he pulled into a parking lot. "That's all I'm going to be thinking of all day!"

Dillon laughed, turned off the ignition and then bent to kiss her. "Maybe the image of running from the teacher wielding a paddle..." he paused, remembering that she'd said one of her hard limits was a wooden paddle. "Sorry, babe—"

"No, don't be," she said softly, reaching up to cup his cheek. "I trust you and know that you'd never harm me." She bent forward and kissed him lightly.

He helped her out of the truck and clipped a leash onto Lucy's collar. "We've got some time to get you checked in and look around before the others arrive."

Dillon took her into a building and introduced her to several people he worked with. He wasn't the least bit surprised when the teasing ended and she turned into the serious agent he'd met all those months ago. He also wasn't surprised that she seemed to be absorbing everything as he gave her a quick tour on the way to his office. Once inside, he gathered the papers he'd need as she looked around.

"You have some pretty impressive accolades, Special Agent MacAllister." He glanced up from the papers on a clipboard he was flipping through to see her standing at the wall where several plaques hung.

"I've worked with some great teams," he said, not one to be particularly impressed by what he considered an expected, but unnecessary, ego-wall.

"You forget; I've seen you in action. I think it's wonderful that you not only do what you do, but that you train others to do it as well. The more thoroughly trained any agent is, the better it is for the good guys."

He accepted her compliment and then led her back out into the hall. "Come on, I've got a little shopping to do."

"More shopping? What kind of shopping?" she asked, suspicion in her voice.

Dillon chuckled and bent down to whisper, "Did I forget to mention we have a training area on researching new products for that special course I told you about?"

Her eyes widened and her mouth opened before her nose crinkled. "You are so bad."

"And you love every minute of it," he said, leading her down another hall and into a large locker room. "It's going to be sunny and I don't want you to burn," he said, selecting a baseball cap from a shelf. Loosening the band, he put it on her head and then chuckled as the pouf of hair on top of her head caused the hat to stick up. Removing it, he pulled the band from her hair, smoothing it down and tucking it behind her ears, before adjusting the snaps to fit. "There goes my nifty handle. Guess you'll have to climb up that wall yourself, Fullerton, but at least now you look like an official trainee." She'd paired a polo shirt with the khaki shorts, the DEA emblem over her left breast.

"This group consists of DEA and FBI agents, as well as law enforcement officers from around the country. They've been training for several weeks and will graduate on Friday if all goes well."

She nodded as they left the building behind, and after he'd left Lucy with another agent, he said, "She'll join the other dogs until later. Are you ready to meet the others?"

"Absolutely!"

Dillon and Charlie walked some distance and had just climbed a small rise when she halted. "Wow, you weren't kidding, that's some course!"

Off in the distance was an obstacle course that spread out of sight. He grinned. "Having second thoughts, Agent Fullerton?"

She smiled and shook her head. "Are you kidding? I can't wait!"

Dillon laughed as she kept looking towards the obstacle course as he led her down the small hill to where people were milling about. Like the both of them, the dozen who made up the class were all in shorts, and shirts with various emblems denoting their agency on their chests. All wore baseball caps as well.

"Morning," Dillon said.

"Good morning, Sir," they all replied, the chatter stopping as they formed a line in front of him.

"I'd like to introduce you to Agent Fullerton. She's DEA working down in Texas. She's going to join us for the rest of the week." He looked down the line and grinned. "Couple of things you need to know. Don't let her size fool you, she's little but she can have you flat on your back before you can blink. And, don't embarrass me by letting her outshine you, because I assure you, she's gonna try."

"Gee thanks," Charlie muttered, knowing her face was heating.

Dillon just grinned knowing that if she had intended to hold back, she wouldn't dare now.

"Now, get in line, recruit!" A slap against her shorts had her jumping and her face coloring, and yet she was wearing a huge smile.

Once she had joined the others, the line moved into two, spreading out, and Dillon began to lead them through exercises that would get their blood pumping and their muscles loosening. He was a man who believed in teaching by example. Though he could easily assign some assistant to lead them through their paces, he exercised right along with him. He might pay a hefty monthly fee to be a member of Black Light, but he didn't have to pay a dime for a gym. He pushed his body hard, the reward being not only physical fitness, but an endurance that allowed him to play and a stamina that assured that play could go for hours. Hours he hoped would extend into years if he could convince a little Texan to join him.

* * *

CHARLIE JUMPED, bent, stretched, did sit ups and crunches with the rest of them, feeling the pull of muscles and yet reveling in the exercise. After their 'little warm-up', Dillon instructed them to hydrate and handed her a bottle of water. It became clear that he wasn't hung up on his position as the others milled around them, welcoming her and joking with Dillon. She was surprised when one of the other DEA agents congratulated her on the drug bust.

"Thanks, it was only possible because of agents like y'all. Dill… I mean, Special Agent MacAllister and Lucy spent several months training DEA and ICE agents before the operation. The K-9 corps were responsible for leading us to the drugs. It was absolutely amazing to watch the dogs work."

"Ahhh, so it was really Lucy who captured your heart?" Claudia, a female FBI agent asked.

"Um, I think I'll keep that a secret," Charlie said, knowing her face had heated as she saw Dillon grin. The group's easy banter and camaraderie allowed Charlie not only to relax but to feel more a part of the group as they easily accepted her as a fellow agent.

"Okay, enough chit-chat," Dillon said. "Remember to hydrate at the stations. Pace yourselves, but just to keep you motivated, the last one to the course will pay a penalty. All right, move out."

Charlie ran beside the others, enjoying the sight of Dillon in the lead. He was by far the most fit man she'd ever seen. His muscles rippled as he ran, his long stride easily eating up the miles as the group ran, and his butt... she could look at it flexing all day. Unlike the recruits she'd seen earlier running on the grounds, Dillon led them not over a road, but through the trees. As the first mile passed and then the second, the group began to spread apart. Not about to discover what the penalty was for being last, Charlie stayed in the middle. The run was taxing, but it was beautiful. Unlike the parts of Texas where she'd worked, which was basically flat, there were rolling hills and rises that they ran up and down. She could see the blue of a lake off in the distance and the grass was a verdant green. By the fifth mile, she was beginning to feel the strain in both her legs and her lungs, a bit surprised but realized that she was running at a higher elevation as well. She fell back a little, but not enough to be in last place. As they passed a juncture, she saw those ahead veering to the right to grab a water bottle from a large plastic bin. Doing the same, she continued to run as she gulped down most of the icy cold liquid and then upended the remainder at the back of her neck. She shuddered and her nipples hardened inside her sports bra at the sudden shock, but felt refreshed enough to pick up the pace. It wasn't long before she found a burst of energy as the obstacle course came into view. Though she was breathing hard by the time she joined the others, she wasn't last.

"Good job," Dillon said, handing her another bottle of water. "Drink all of it."

"Yes, Sir," she said, saluting him with the bottle before uncapping it.

"Smartass," he said softly, grinning as he did.

A few minutes later, she heard him say, "Nice of you to join us, Baxter. Drop and give me fifty."

"Yes, Sir," the man said. He was an FBI agent who'd joined the K-9 corps upon successful completion of the basic agent training course and didn't bat an eye as he began to pay the penalty for being last. The muscles in his biceps bulged as he pressed his body weight up and down, nose to the ground with each descent. It didn't take him long either. For the last push-up, he folded an arm across his back and after he completed it, he jumped to his feet.

"Well done," Charlie said, passing him a bottle of water. "You made that look so easy."

Baxter chuckled and drained the bottle in one long swallow. "Beats having to run fast."

They lined up into two teams to run the course. "Remember, you're a team and only as strong as your weakest link. Help each other through," Dillon instructed.

Charlie was on his team and their group took off to run the course on the left as the other group headed towards the right. She lifted her knees high to step through the tires and then dropped to her belly to crawl beneath a set of ropes that allowed only a few inches of clearance. She watched the person in front of her stumble and then fall from a balance beam, encouraging him to try again. Once he succeeded, he watched as she flew across the narrow beam and jumped off the other end.

"Impressive," he said.

"Smaller feet," she countered, as Dillon landed beside them.

She swung from bars and grabbed the rope as it was swung back to her after a team mate cleared a large mud puddle. She grabbed hold, swung and then squealed as she made it less than halfway across before swinging back. Hands grabbed her, saving her from falling into the mud. She heard Dillon behind her. "This is where teamwork comes in. Hang on and don't let go." He grabbed her and she clung to his back like a monkey as he grabbed the rope, moved back and took off at a full run. She buried her face in his neck as they left the ground, not believing that Dillon, was actually making the same yodeling sound that reminded her of movies she'd watched as a teen.

They landed with a jolt and she took a moment to give him a hug. "Thanks, Tarzan," she said as she slid from his back. The team jumped hurdles and crawled beneath lower bars and then came to the first wall only a few seconds ahead of the other team. "Whoa, it looks a lot bigger up close," Charlie said, her head craned back to see the top of the wall. Baxter ran, planted his feet and leapt, catching the lip of the wall on his first try and pulled himself up. He turned and as the others followed, he'd catch their hands and pull them up.

"Your turn," Dillon asked.

"Here goes," she said, running towards the wall as fast as she could. When she leapt, her hands came nowhere near Baxter's or the other agent reaching down to help. Instead, she slid down the wall and fell on her butt.

"Still having fun?" Dillon asked, reaching down to help her to her feet.

"A blast," she said, her hands rubbing her ass. She tried again, coming closer but still falling short. "Damn!" she exclaimed, looking over to see the other team's last member being hauled up and over.

"Come on, Fullerton! You can do it!"

Looking back, she said, "How about demonstrating that teamwork, Sir?"

"Thought you'd never ask, recruit," Dillon said, his eyebrows wagging and causing her to need to take an extra moment to draw in a deep breath. She took off again, but this time, when she didn't quite reach the fingers extended towards her, she felt very familiar palms cupping her ass and lifting her up, giving a few unnecessary squeezes in the process. Her hands were grabbed and she was pulled over, turning back in time to see Dillon make it over easily, his grin telling of his enjoyment of copping a feel.

She just shook her head at him and turned to the others. "Sorry, guys," she apologized.

"No worries," Baxter said, "we can catch them."

It was the most challenging course she'd ever run and the most fun. She flew over every bridge and shimmied up the rock wall, arriving at the top first and then turning to verbally guide her teammates to hand and foot holds. The group gathered at the next area, and took a moment to strategize. The goal was to climb a rope and ring the bell at the top. But, that bell could not be rung until every member was on the rope.

"I'm not very good with ropes," Charlie admitted.

"That's why you go first," Dillon said. "You're small and can brace your feet on my shoulders, and I'll help push you up." The others agreed and Charlie was thrilled when she reached the top, looked down to see her team on the rope and she rang the bell before the opposing team had their members on the rope. One by one, her teammates dropped to the ground and when Dillon called out, "I've got you," she simply trusted that he would catch her and let go of the rope.

It was a race to the finish. "Oh my God, really?" Charlie said, staring at the huge expanse in front of her. "This is twice as tall as the other."

"And requires strategy," Dillon said, motioning for the team to assemble and allowing them to plot how best to beat the obstacle. Charlie listened as it was explained that each team member had to be on the wall before one climbed over the top.

"Claudia, you'll go first and Charlie, you'll go last. The rest of us will form a ladder," Baxter instructed and at the nods from his teammates, they began to form the human chain. Claudia climbed onto another agents' shoulders and they leaned against the slight incline of the wall as the man put one foot at a time on the next man's shoulders. Inch by inch, they lengthened their ladder until Dillon was the last standing and bearing the weight of the rest.

"Okay, little monkey, shimmy up."

Charlie couldn't resist, giving his buttocks a quick squeeze, loving his chuckle of surprise before she did exactly as he'd instructed. She used any foot- and handhold she could find, shoulders, backs, butts, even heads found her tennis shoe planted for the time it took for her to find her next hold. Once she gripped the rim, she hauled herself over, turned and began helping pull the others up. Baxter and Dillon seemed so distant and yet they grinned and were soon scaling the wall, grabbing for the hands that would pull them the last foot or so. The team staggered across the finish line, whooping like they'd won the gold medal at the Olympics. They cheered the other team on until the entire class collapsed onto the ground, chests heaving, bodies covered in sweat, water, dirt, and mud.

"God, that was fun! Thanks guys," Charlie said, sitting up to drink what was probably her fifth bottle of water since the course had begun.

After they cooled off, they walked/jogged back towards the buildings, to clean up. Dillon handed her a set of shorts and a t-shirt at the door to the women's locker. "Sorry, I forgot to remind you to bring a change of clothing."

"Thanks, these are great!"

She took a quick shower with the other two females in the class. "And to think, we have to do it all over again tomorrow," Claudia groaned as she stepped under the shower spray.

"I can't wait!" Charlie said, earning herself a wet washcloth splatting onto her breasts.

"You're a masochist, Fullerton," Elaine said.

Charlie laughed and tossed the washcloth back. "I suppose so, but really, it was fun."

After they emerged, they did eat in the cafeteria, and Charlie ate every single bite that Dillon put on her tray. She listened to the others talk about their jobs, and heard the pride in each voice about the choice they'd made to go into the K-9 corps. The story Elaine told had her sitting on the edge of her seat as she explained that her older brother had been with the teams searching for survivors after the tsunami that devastated Japan, wiping out an entire city. "He told me it is an emotionally taxing job but finding just one survivor makes all the horrors worthwhile."

Charlie watched in amazement as they went to get their canine partners. Whereas Lucy had been bouncing and playful that morning, the moment Dillon put on the vest that designated her as a K-9 dog, the German Shepherd seemed to stand taller, her ears pointed, her stance one that told of her readiness to work.

For the rest of the afternoon, Charlie didn't actively participate, but she couldn't take her eyes off as the pairs of humans and dogs worked. She followed along a different obstacle course, watching the animals maneuver through tunnels, crawl under obstacles and leap over others. Signals were given to the Shepherds both verbally and by hand. Though she'd witnessed K-9s working before down in Texas, it was still extremely impressive.

When they moved to an area where there was nothing but rubble, she listened as Dillon explained they were searching for bodies. "Split up and go over every inch. Mark what you and your partner deem as a find. Trust your partner. And remember, be careful. The rubble isn't secure." Instead of working with his class, Dillon and Lucy stood by Charlie, observing. By the time the exercise was over, he nodded.

"Baxter, you're the only one who didn't plant a flag. Why?"

"I didn't want to have others waste time in removing the rubble for nothing, Sir."

"And your partner? Does Casper agree?"

Baxter looked down at his dog and back at the rubble. "He seemed to signal, but was hesitant."

Dillon walked forward and pointed towards the area the team had been searching. "No, Baxter. You were just hesitant to trust him. Try again."

After ten minutes, the agent pulled the flag from his pocket and planted it in the rubble. Dillon nodded. "Good job. Baxter, you're only off by a couple of feet." Charlie was impressed with the way Dillon taught, guiding without being condescending. Baxter praised Casper and Dillon turned to the rest of the class. "Elaine, you and Pete did great as the body you've marked is six feet under rock, metal and dirt. All right, that's it for the day."

Charlie watched as the team assembled and spent a half-hour praising and playing with their canine partner. It was obvious that bonds had already developed and she knew would continue to grow stronger between each pair. After the animals had been returned to the kennels, each owner feeding and watering their dog, Dillon removed Lucy's vest and Charlie knelt to give her an extra hug or two.

"That was amazing," she said as they climbed into the truck.

"You were amazing," Dillon said, reaching to pull her onto his lap, cupping her face and planting a kiss on her lips that had her squirming and giving a moan. They broke apart when Lucy decided it should be a group hug, her body weight causing Dillon to break off the kiss and the tongue bath she gave them both had them laughing and pushing her away.

"Okay, okay," Dillon said. "Message received." Charlie slid off his lap and leaned against his arm as they drove through the gates.

Once they were back at the farm and had fed and run the puppies through their exercise, Charlie's steps were slower as they entered the house. "Remember last night?" she asked as she climbed the steps of the porch.

"Babe, I'm not likely to ever forget last night."

His answer had her smiling as she'd never forget it either, but that wasn't her point. "Good, because I'm aching all over and could sure use a very thorough massage."

"That I can do," Dillon said, sweeping her off her feet and carrying her up the stairs. She not only got her massage, moaning as he kneaded every inch of her, she returned the favor. Pressing hands into his skin, tracing his muscles, listening to him give grunts of pleasure as she straddled his naked butt and put all of her weight into it. She squealed as he turned over, grabbed her and had her beneath him in the blink of an eye.

He slid into her and she found the strength to wrap around him, pulling him closer, lifting her hips, meeting every thrust until they both came. Dillon collapsed onto his back and pulled her close. Charlie snuggled into him as she regained her breath, feeling more content than she had ever before, and yet even though she was exhausted, she laid awake a long time, listening to Dillon's even breathing. How was she ever going to be able to leave him? She'd worked hard to prove herself, to move up to a position of authority within the DEA. She'd never considered moving out of Texas... until now. She could no longer deny that what she'd both dreamed and feared had happened. She'd fallen in love—head over heels in love—with Dillon MacAllister. But she was still not sure he was thinking beyond this week or feeling anything remotely like she was. When he pulled her a bit closer, she entwined her fingers with his, needing the connection and praying that she'd find the answer she so desperately needed.

CHAPTER 12

*T*he week passed quickly. By the time Thursday arrived, Charlie could swing across the mud pit without help and though she still needed assistance scaling even the first wall, the others considered her a true member of their team. When they gathered in front of a huge warehouse, she felt incredibly honored when Dillon stepped forward and offered her Lucy's leash.

"You're DEA and you can do this. You've learned the signals. Lead the team in, Charlie."

She had and led the others through the dimly lit interior, searching through junk and clutter, going into offices, trusting Lucy to guide her. The team spent an hour searching every inch and by the time she called a cease to the exercise, dozens of little flags marked hidden caches of narcotics.

"Excellent," Dillon said, checking their markers against a diagram in his hand. "I am extremely proud of all of you. It will be my honor to give you your certificates at the ceremony tomorrow."

On Friday, Charlie didn't wear her shorts or shirt. Instead, she wore the pumpkin colored dress and stood, with tears in her eyes, applauding as each person, their dog at their side, walked proudly across the stage. She watched Dillon shake each of their hands, squatting to pet and praise their furry partner and hand them certificates of graduation.

She joined the family and friends of the graduates at the reception. Dillon spoke with everyone, praising his trainees to their loved ones. Claudia came over and gave Charlie a hug. "Are you really going back to Texas?"

"Yes, tomorrow," Charlie said.

"Remember the first day and I asked it if had been Lucy to steal your heart?"

"Yes," Charlie said again.

"Charlie, you are one of the most observant people I've ever met. You learned hand signals in less time than the rest of us. And yet, you obviously can't see what's right before your eyes."

Charlie looked up at her. "What do you mean?"

"Girl, if you can't see that MacAllister is in love with you, you aren't nearly as observant as I believed." Charlie was surprised as other than a few swats on her ass when he was behind her, and a few kisses once in the privacy of the truck, they'd kept it professional, yet her heart leapt at Claudia's words. Could they be true?

Claudia just shook her head. "And, if you think I don't know you are just as crazy about him, then, well... I honestly don't know what to think."

"I love him," Charlie said, realizing it was the first time she'd said the words out loud. "But... he hasn't said he feels the same."

Claudia laughed. "Charlie, that man says it every single time he looks at you. We all saw it the first day and every day since. You know how Dillon is constantly reminding us to trust our partner? To rely on their senses?" Charlie nodded, having heard it several times. "Then, Charlie, trust your heart. You'll be making the biggest mistake of your life if you don't." She paused and then smiled. "And though I still think you are slightly insane for enjoying putting yourself through the grind of the courses, I am very honored to have met you and consider you a friend."

Charlie felt tears welling and reached out to hug the woman. "Thank you, Claudia. I consider it an honor to be your friend."

"Ready to go?" Dillon asked a bit later.

Though she knew he wasn't asking about tomorrow, she couldn't help but wonder was she? Ready to return to Texas? But, that's not what she said. Instead, she fell back on what was easy... what didn't threaten to consume her. "Aren't we going to stay and eat?" Charlie said as people began moving towards tables where a buffet had been set up.

"I thought we'd take that horseback ride before it gets too late."

"That sounds perfect," Charlie agreed honestly, slipping her hand into his, no longer concerned if anyone saw. The drive through the gates had her turning to look back. "Thank you, Dillon. I'll never forget this past week."

He dropped his arm around her shoulders, pulling her close and dropping a kiss on top of her head. "Neither will I. It's been the most incredible week of my life, Charlie. I won't forget a single moment since I looked up and saw you standing in the club."

Could that be true? She felt the exact same way and yet still held back, still unsure of herself. Once home, she ran upstairs to change and then she climbed on the back of an ATV for the ride out to the stables.

"Janet has picked Beauty for you to ride," he said as he led her into the barn.

Charlie smiled. "And you're riding Beast?"

Dillon chuckled. "No, my mount's name is Buster." Charlie giggled and after they'd saddled the horses, he led the way out of the barn.

"Wait, where's the picnic basket?" she asked realizing she'd yet to see one.

"You'll see," Dillon said. "Now, Tex, let's see what sort of rider you are." With a touch of his boots against his horse's flanks, Buster took off. Charlie smiled and took off after him. They raced across fields and over rises, her hair whipping wildly. She pulled ahead and when she felt Beauty's muscles bunch, she leaned forward across the horse's neck and they sailed over a fence. She hadn't ridden in months and yet she felt as one with her mount. As they raced across the fields, she felt her churning thoughts beginning to settle, flashes of the days she'd spent with Dillon playing across her mind. The sense of impending panic dissipated with the very beauty of her surroundings. This wasn't a time to dread... it was a time to soak up every moment she had left... to store them in her mind and her heart, to take out and live again and again.

They began to slow to allow the horses to rest and Dillon drew up close to her. "That was wonderful, Dillon, thank you."

He smiled and leaned over to kiss her. "You might ride like the wind, Tex, but you'll always be my yellow Rose." Her heart hitched but before she could speak, he gestured ahead to a grove of trees. "Dinner awaits, my lady."

As they drew nearer, Charlie smiled as she saw the patchwork quilt spread across the grass, a big picnic basket in the center. Dillon dismounted and lifted her from the saddle, slowly sliding her down his body, igniting her arousal instantly. When her feet hit the ground, she wrapped her arms around him, inhaling deeply of his scent, knowing that if she were blindfolded, in a room of a thousand people, she'd be able to find the one man by simply sniffing the air. She smiled wondering if perhaps she'd spent a bit too much time with the dogs and then forgot that thought the moment Dillon lifted her chin and bent to kiss her until her insides were liquid.

Dillon let the horses roam, telling her they'd come when he called and she had no doubt they would. He had an affinity with animals that amazed her. Janet had packed fried chicken, potato salad, baked beans and deviled eggs. Dillon handed containers to Charlie and then handed her a wine glass, and then another.

"Well, looks like we have glasses but nothing to drink," he said after rummaging in the basket for another moment.

Charlie peeled off a small piece of paper that had been taped to the bottom of one of the glasses. "Janet says to look in the water."

Dillon glanced up towards the pond. "Smart girl," he said, walking to the water. Charlie watched as he squatted and pulled on a rope. "Very smart girl," he said, returning with a smile on his face and a bottle of wine in his hand. "That explains the corkscrew." He opened the wine while Charlie loaded their plates with the food. They chatted about the beauty surrounding them and the fun of the horseback ride. After he'd gone back to the basket and served her a huge slice of chocolate cake, it was delicious but far too much for her stomach which felt as if the butterflies they'd watched flitting about the field had settled inside. Looking up, she found Dillon's eyes on her.

"Dillon…"

"Charlie…" they said at the same time. "You first," he said.

Charlie looked away and then looked into his eyes. "Remember the last time we were at Lupitos?" He nodded and she took another breath. "You asked me to take a serious look at my life. You asked questions that I'd been avoiding for a long time. But, what you really did was plant a seed." She took another breath and knew that no matter the outcome, it was time to push aside her doubts, her fears and speak from her heart. "The night at Black Light, that seed germinated and every day, every moment spent with you, it has grown. I- I don't want to leave you. I ache all over with the thought of not being here… with you. I love you, Dillon."

"Thank God!" Dillon said, tossing his plate aside and taking hers before pulling her into his arms. "You just saved my director a heart attack."

Charlie looked up. "Your director?"

"Yes. Do you know how many state lines I'd be crossing when I followed you to Texas only to drag you back to Virginia? It would be quite embarrassing for my director to have to defend me against kidnapping charges." He smiled and then bent to kiss her, but when they parted, she had one more question.

"Why didn't you say something?" she asked.

"Every time I touched you, held you, kissed you, I thought I was showing you. I thought you knew. I was an idiot."

"No, not an idiot." She grinned and shook her head, adding, "But perhaps a man used to communicating with dogs who don't need words."

He kissed her again, pulling her to him. "Definitely an idiot. I should have realized that words are just as important... even more so than signals. From now on, no more assumptions. Not about anything. Both of us will be open and honest. I'm sorry I didn't just come out and tell you, sweetheart. I love you more than I've ever dreamed it possible to love another."

With those words, that instruction, his kiss, she knew she was exactly where she was supposed to be.

When he moved to reach for the basket, she groaned.

"Dillon, I can't possibly eat another bite."

He didn't even look up as he pulled something from the basket. When he came to her again, he dropped to one knee. "I love you, Charlize Elena Fullerton. I've loved you for months and can't imagine waking up without you beside me. Marry me, Charlie. Marry me and make me the happiest man on earth. Make Virginia your home... with me."

"Yes!" Charlie said, allowing the tears she'd been holding to fall as he opened the small box to reveal a beautiful solitaire.

"This was my grandmother Ruby's ring. She would have loved you, Charlie, and I know you would have adored her." He slipped it onto her ring finger and then kissed it before drawing her into his arms again. "You are both wonderful women who have filled my heart with love."

"That's a beautiful thought. I'll wear it with pride and can't wait to hear more stories about your grandmother."

Then Dillon slowly undressed her and she him until he laid her back on the quilt. They made love that brought fresh tears to her eyes.

"Don't cry, baby," Dillon said, bending to kiss her cheeks.

"I can't help it, I'm so happy," she said, pulling him to her, their kiss as gentle as their love making and yet it filled both her heart and her soul.

* * *

"You call me every time you stop," Dillon said, giving her yet another reminder.

"I will. And yes, I'll stop every couple of hours and stretch my legs. Of course, you do realize that will make my trip longer?" she teased.

"A few hours longer is worth you arriving safely," Dillon said, loading the last of her stuff into her Tahoe.

"He's right. We want you back in one piece," Martha said, hugging her. "We've got a wedding to plan you know."

"A simple wedding," Charlie said. "I don't need anything flashy. I just want you and Owen and a few others. All that matters is that I'll be Dillon's wife." She paused and looked down at her hand where the diamond sparkled. "Wife, wow! I'm still shocked."

"Happily shocked, I hope," Dillon said, taking her back into his arms. "God, I'm going to miss you."

"I'll be back before you know it. I've already talked to my captain and he knows I've put in for a transfer. In a couple of weeks, I'll be a real trainee."

Dillon wagged his eyebrow. "And I'll be your teacher, which reminds me—"

Charlie slapped his chest. "I am not going to come to class in a plaid skirt and knee socks."

Martha laughed. "I don't know, that might be fun, but don't forget, Dillon, naughty school girls are supposed to wear their hair in pigtails and have white granny panties—"

"That's it. The next time you're at the club, I'm going to put a gag in your mouth and show you that topping from the bottom is NOT acceptable."

Charlie watched as Marty turned to look up at Owen. "Can it be a red ball? That way it will match these new panties I bought? And can we start out on the spanking bench? But I don't want you to spank too hard—" her voice trailed off as Owen growled and Dillon rolled his eyes.

"And on that note, I've got to get on the road," Charlie said. She gave hugs to both Martha and Owen and bent to give Lucy a hug.

"You take care of our guy, okay?"

Lucy gave a single woof and licked her cheek before Charlie stood and stepped into Dillon's arms.

"You be careful, babe. Don't drive all day. Call me often and when you stop for the night."

"I will. I love you, Dillon."

"I love you, Charlie. I love you with all my heart. Now, lift up your shirt."

"What?"

"How quickly you forget I'm not only your fiancé, I'm your Dom. Lift up your shirt."

Charlie did so, pulling her t-shirt free of her shorts and holding it to bare her stomach. Her heart lurched when Dillon pulled two lengths of white rope from his pocket.

"This is you," he said, holding up one piece. "And this is me." He put them around her waist and began to weave the ropes, intertwining them in a simple but beautiful pattern. "Though we are apart, we are connected." She watched as he began to tie a knot that rested against her naval. "Don't take this off," he said, bending to kiss the knot before taking her shirt from her hand and covering the rope.

"I won't," she said, cupping his face with her palms. "God, I love you, Sir."

"I love you, too. Be safe, but hurry and come back home to me." He kissed her until her knees were weak and then helped her into the car.

Even though Charlie was leaving him, the rope around her waist kept her connected, the promise of the shibari they'd share filling her head and her love for him filling her heart.

* * *

THEY SPOKE OFTEN as she drove through states and for hours as she checked into various hotels at night. On the fourth day, she arrived at the house where she rented a room. Tomorrow she'd pack what few belongings she'd take back with her, donating the rest to Goodwill. She'd report in at work on Wednesday and begin the paperwork that would transfer her to the K-9 corps of the DEA.

She climbed into bed that night and waited for her call to connect.

"Hello, my love."

Charlie smiled as she heard Dillon's voice. "Hi. How was your day?"

"Better now that I'm talking to you. Seriously, how are you feeling?"

"A little tired, but glad that I'm a day closer to coming back to you."

"Are you in bed?" When she said she was, he asked, "What are you wearing?"

"Just your shirt and our belt, Sir."

"That's too much clothing. Put the phone on speaker, take off the shirt and lie back."

Charlie felt her body quicken with his instructions. She set the phone beside her, pulled off the t-shirt she'd worn to bed every night, and lay back, her hand going to the knot on her stomach.

"Spread your legs apart." He paused and then said, "Wider."

She smiled and obeyed, spreading her legs wide, feeling the coil beginning to wind inside her.

"Massage your breasts," he instructed, guiding her through the massage until her nipples were hard and demanding to be touched. As if he could see, his next order was to play with her nipples.

She moved her fingers towards her nipples, but before she could take them, Dillon's voice came through the speaker.

"Lick your fingers first. Put them in your mouth and suck, like you do my cock." Her pussy spasmed as she obeyed, closing her eyes, memories of her lips stretched around his cock playing in her mind as she suckled on her fingers. She gave a soft moan, and Dillon said, "That's my girl. Now, play with your nipples."

She obeyed, the wetness of her saliva transferred to her taut buds as she rolled and pinched her nipples. "Harder, Charlie. I want to hear you moan. Pinch them as I would."

The room filled with the sounds of her moans as she tugged and twisted on the sensitive nubs. Several minutes passed before he spoke again.

"Are you wet, Charlie? Is your pussy pulsing?"

"Yes... yes, Sir," she said softly.

"Keep playing with your nipples but put one hand between your legs. Don't touch your clit, spread those beautiful rose petals apart." She obeyed and gasped as her fingers slid through her sex, her moisture making them slide so easily as she spread her lips open. She stroked the soft skin, feeling her clit jump, her lips swell.

"Don't forget your nipples," Dillon said with a chuckle. Charlie blushed, again wondering how he knew she'd forgotten them in her play. She gave each one an extra hard pinch, gasping with each one and yet feeling more of her essence slip from her pussy.

"Two fingers, inside now." He gave her a moment and then asked, "Are they inside your cunt, Charlie?"

"Ye-yes, Sir."

"Good girl. I want you to finger fuck yourself, in and out, start slow and then hard and fast. Do not touch your clit."

She began to move her fingers in and out of her pussy, wishing it was Dillon's cock with each thrust. Her hand moved from breast to breast, tugging, twisting and pinching her nipples as the spring coiled tighter.

"Charlie?"

"Ye... yes?"

"Is your clittie pulsing, throbbing, out of its hood demanding to be touched?"

"God, yes, Sir. May I touch it, Sir?"

"No, not yet. Add another finger to your pussy." She did, moaning as her vagina stretched to accept the additional digit. "I love hearing every gasp, every breath as you fuck yourself for me. I can picture you lying there, your legs spread wide, your fingers in your cunt driving in and out, filling that sweet, hot pussy."

"Oh, God, please... please, Sir, I need to come."

"Keep those fingers in your pussy. Take your other hand and play with your clit. Come for me, Charlie. Let me hear your pleasure."

Charlie's fingers played and within moments she was arching off the mattress as the coil sprung, a burst of pleasure flooding her senses. She whimpered with the release, wishing so much that Dillon was in the room with her.

"That was beautiful, Charlie. I love you."

"I love you, too, Dillon."

"Sweet dreams, my love. I'll talk to you tomorrow."

"Good night, Dillon."

She pulled her hands from her sex, and rolled to her side, pulling the shirt she'd discarded to her chest, hugging it as she shut off the phone and dreamed of a man over a thousand miles away.

CHAPTER 13

*D*illon paced his office as he listened to the phone ring again, and again and again. He pressed the end call button and felt the sick feeling in his gut grow larger. Though Charlie should have been back by now, she'd been asked to return to Brownsville. She'd apologized, but even though he was disappointed, he understood she felt a sense of duty.

"I won't lie and say I'm thrilled, but I understand, Charlie," he had said. "It will give you the closure you need to be able to leave Texas behind. But, promise me, you'll be careful. I don't trust that sonofabitch as far as I can throw him."

"He's in custody, Dillon."

"I know, honey, but still, I'm not very happy that all of a sudden Sorenson is offering information. Why insist it was you he talk to? It's suspicious to me."

"I don't know, maybe he feels remorse for what he's done. But if the information he provides helps us stop or even slow the flow of drugs across the border, not to mention the young women pulled into his trap, a few days will be worth it. I'll be careful," she promised. "Once it's over, I'll be on my way home. I love you, Dillon."

"Home. Now that I am very happy about. I love you, too. Call me as often as you can."

She'd promised, and he knew she wouldn't break her word. Something was wrong... something was very wrong. He was scrolling through his contacts when the phone rang.

"Charlie? Thank God. Are you all right?"

"Special Agent MacAllister?"

Instead of Charlie's voice, a much deeper tone came over the phone and his gut twisted. "This is he, who is this?"

"This is Captain Morrow—"

"What's wrong? Where's Charlie?" Dillon demanded.

"Sorenson gave us information that we were able to confirm about a tunnel running between Brownsville and Matamoros. He told us of the next scheduled run—but it was a trap. We're not sure how it was arranged but it was retribution from the cartel for the loss of the drugs and cash we confiscated. A team of agents went in and we lost contact..." He paused and Dillon closed his eyes. "Dillon, they blew the tunnel. The explosion was massive and took out buildings in Matamoros. We've sent teams in and have recovered bodies... but son, Charlize hasn't been found. I'm so sorry to tell you—"

"No!" Dillon said, his eyes snapping open. "Don't you dare fucking say it. She's not dead. I'm on my way!"

"Dillon—"

Dillon was already running out of his office and almost knocked over his director who placed his hand on Dillon's chest and said, "I've just heard—"

"She's not dead!" Dillon said again.

"The jet is fueling and the team is assembling. Go find her; go bring her home."

Within a half-hour, the jet was in the air. A team of five other agents and their canine partners joined him on the flight. Dillon sat, his hand in Lucy's fur as images played through his mind. He was not conscious of the other agents' chatter. Charlie's voice, her laugh, the sound of her moans of pleasure were all he heard. Forcing back the tears that threatened to fall, he drew on the memories of her strength. Charlie was strong, she was a fighter, she wouldn't give up and neither could he. "Hang on, Charlie. I'm coming for you, baby. Just hang on."

The jet landed in Brownsville and Captain Morrow was waiting. Dillon would have slugged him if he'd said that Charlie was gone. He was extremely grateful when the captain just nodded and brought him up to date.

"Teams have been searching since yesterday," Morrow said. "Eight agents went in, five with dogs. Three made it through the tunnel and were recovered from the rubble of the building when it blew. One has since died of his injuries; the others are in critical condition. We've recovered another but he didn't survive. So far we've found ten residents of the town buried in the rubble of the building on the Mexican side."

"Charlie would be in the back," Dillon said. "She'd allow the dogs to go first."

"I agree," Morrow said. "The last contact we had was her stating that Agent Carter with ICE and the K-9 teams had gone in and that she and Officer Cortez were about to enter the tunnel."

"Then that's where we'll start," Dillon said but Morrow reached out and laid his hand on his arm. "The tunnel has continued to collapse at both ends. It's over a mile and runs under the river. God knows how the fuck they ever built it, but it's not stable and though we're working on shoring it up, it's not safe. There are continuous tremors. Divers have gone down but visibility is poor. So far we haven't found signs of the roof collapsing, but if it does, the tunnel will flood. A team has been running FINDER, the ground-penetrating radar. Dillon, they detected a faint heartbeat... but the signal disappeared a few hours ago."

"I don't give a fuck. Any number of things could interfere with their readings," Dillon said. "Lucy will find her. We start where Charlie and the others went in."

174

Morrow nodded and led the team to waiting helicopters.

Dillon began issuing directions but a man stepped forward. "You're not going in alone." It was Baxter, the newest member of the corps, joining after graduation of the course he'd run with Charlie.

"You heard Morrow, it's not safe. I won't risk—"

"You'll need help to find Charlie. The rest of the team can begin in Matamoros, but I need to go with you." Dillon nodded, knowing Baxter was as aware of the danger as he. His dog, Casper, looked just as determined to join in the search. It took only a few minutes to fly the distance from the airport to a clearing near a few ramshackle buildings.

"The tunnel entrance is in the third building," Morrow said though Dillon wasn't looking in that direction. Instead, his eyes locked on Charlie's Tahoe.

"Just a minute," Dillon said, moving towards the car. He had just picked up a rock to break the window when an officer stopped him, pulling a tool from his belt. Within seconds, he'd worked the bar and popped the lock. Dillon grabbed Charlie's suitcase, unzipping it and searching inside. He pulled out the t-shirt he'd given her to wear at night. To feel closer to him. Forcing himself from those thoughts, he bunched the shirt in his hand and squatted in front of Lucy.

"Find her, Lucy. Find our girl." The dog sniffed the shirt and then the air. Dillon led her to the building and inside.

Morrow hadn't been kidding. The tunnel was full of debris though teams had been working to clear it for hours. As he moved forward, he kept away from the walls, the knowledge that they could collapse in his mind and yet he continued. He and Baxter had to halt several times to help clear debris, waiting as teams worked to shore up the walls. It was slow work. It was dirty. It was tedious and physically exhausting. If it was this bad on the American side, he couldn't imagine how bad the damage was closer to the source of the explosion. Hours passed and yet Dillon and Baxter refused to retreat. Charlie was in here somewhere waiting for him to find her.

They'd begun a decline and Dillon knew they had to be under the Rio Grande but tried not to think of the river running above him. When Lucy signaled, his heart clutched. It wasn't the signal that she'd found a survivor, it was one given when a corpse had been detected. It took the two men a half-hour to dig through the layer of debris before the body became visible. Though his heart began to beat again at the realization that it wasn't Charlie, he still mourned. "It's Alejandro," he said, sending the information through the radios they had to use since they were so far underground. "He didn't make it."

Dillon accepted a bottle of water, pouring some into his hands for Lucy to lap as they waited for a team to remove the body. The moment they moved past him back down the tunnel, he and Lucy moved forward. His gut told him that Charlie wouldn't be far. He dug, he moved rocks, he shifted wood and chunks of concrete that had been used to add additional support for the part of the tunnel that ran under the river.

A rumble sounded and he signaled for Baxter to stop, praying that the tremor wasn't enough to cause another cave in. The only light came from their high power flashlights, motes of dust visible as they shimmered in the air. When the sound faded, the walls still holding, he pushed on. Lucy signaled again and for the first time, the dog whined and strained at the leash.

"Easy girl," Dillon said softly. "Good girl... easy now." He dropped to his knees, digging through the dirt. Debris made the tunnel narrow and claustrophobic but he and Baxter worked side by side on their knees.

"Dillon," Baxter said, pointing his light up.

"Fuck," Dillon said as a drop of water fell, followed by another. "Take the dogs and go."

Baxter shook his head and moved another piece of concrete. Five minutes passed, the drip becoming more pronounced as

Dillon's hand brushed dirt away and he saw a boot. "Hang on, Charlie. I've got you, baby." He worked quickly but carefully as more tremors caused small clods of dirt, some very wet to fall from the ceiling. "Just a few more seconds. Hang on."

If Charlie had been any larger, she'd have been crushed. As it was, the beam that had fallen across her body pinned her to what appeared to be a shallow dip in the dirt floor. His hand ran over her legs but she didn't even twitch. She was lying on her back, covered in dirt. He played the light over her. The light bounced off the diamond on her finger but that wasn't what tore at his soul. It was the fact that the fingers of her left hand were curled around the knot of the rope he'd tied around her waist.

"Oh, Charlie, baby, I'm here, you're going to be all right. Just hang on."

There was so little space to maneuver, and yet Baxter slithered on his belly, braced his back beneath the beam and lifted it a few inches, every muscle straining with the effort. "Now," he said. There was no room to lift her and Dillon cringed when he began to pull her towards him, knowing the move could cause more injury but he had no choice. He heard the best sound in the world when she whimpered.

"I know, baby. I know it hurts but you're going to be okay. Just hang on." He had to slide her quickly as the beam was heavy and awkward for his partner to hold.

The moment he got her clear, Baxter crawled backwards, a far deeper rumble put urgency in his voice. "Fuck, it's going to collapse."

Baxter unclipped the leashes from their dogs' collars. "Go!" he directed, giving the signal. Casper immediately responded but when Lucy hesitated, it took Dillon repeating the order to have her turn to follow Casper back the way they'd come. Dillon was as gentle as possible, cradling her body to his chest but knew that every move caused her pain. He was grateful she was unconscious, not wanting her to feel the agony.

Morrow's voice came over the radio. "You need to get out. Divers are reporting breaches. I'm sorry but—"

Baxter radioed that they'd found her. "She's hurt but alive. We're coming."

"Thank God," Morrow said. "For God's sake, hurry!"

The trip back was faster, both due to the additional clearing and shoring the team had done as well as Dillon and Baxter knowing they were living on borrowed time as the rumbles didn't cease.

When Dillon stumbled, Baxter was there to brace him. The two men drew on every ounce of strength they had to get Charlie to safety. They could see daylight and it gave them the last boost as they cleared the tunnel to the cheering of dozens of agents and volunteers. An ambulance was waiting, paramedics coming forward to take Charlie. Dillon laid her carefully on the gurney, bending to kiss her forehead, then stepped back as they loaded her into the back. Dillon watched as Lucy jumped into the ambulance. The paramedic turned and his mouth opened but Dillon spoke as he climbed in. "We're going." He turned and saw Baxter squatting beside Casper, ruffling his fur, the huge smile on Baxter's face stating the sense of victory for the team. Morrow, looking haggard also grinned and nodded before the doors were slammed and the siren began to blare. Dillon reached out and placed his hand on Charlie's leg, not getting in the way of the paramedic who was examining her, but having to touch her, to let her know that he was there.

She was filthy, she was cut, bloodied and bruised, the lower half of her face covered with the oxygen mask the paramedic placed over her head, and yet she had never been more beautiful to him. He bowed his head, allowed the tears to fall, thanking God that he'd not taken the other half of his soul.

* * *

DILLON FOLLOWED the gurney through the emergency room doors, never losing contact with Charlie's leg. He'd watched the paramedics, heard them speaking with the hospital and knew that she was having trouble breathing and that her blood pressure was dangerously low. He felt that as long as he touched her, that somehow she'd know that he was with her, that she wouldn't leave him.

"Sir, I'm going to have to ask you to leave," a nurse said as he followed the team into an examination room.

"No."

"We can't have dogs in here. There's a waiting room—"

"We're staying."

The woman looked at him and then down at Lucy who was sitting at his side. "All right, but you'll need to step back."

That Dillon could do, though it meant he had to remove his hand. He bent over the gurney. "Fight, Charlie. Don't you dare give up. You fight and come back to me." He kissed her and then stepped away to let other professionals do their jobs.

The nurse began to cut Charlie's clothes off and as she cut up the center of the t-shirt, she saw the rope around her waist. Once the shirt was removed, she placed the scissors under the rope. "It was to remind her that we're connected."

Dillon didn't realize he'd spoken aloud until the young woman looked at him. "She knows you're here." He nodded, knowing that somehow Charlie did know. The nurse moved the scissors to Charlie's side and cut through the belt. She slid it free and turned and handed it to Dillon as the door opened and a doctor entered.

"We'll take care of her, I promise," the nurse said.

Dillon nodded again, understanding that his presence was hampering the process. "Lucy, come. Our girl is going to be fine."

He was pacing the floor of the waiting room when Baxter and Morrow arrived. Accepting a cup of coffee, Dillon slumped in a chair and after reporting that he'd heard nothing so far, listened as the captain filled him in.

"Your team recovered Agent Carter. He was brought in before Charlize. We've accounted for everyone we sent in, but if there were more from the Mexican side, the tunnel will be their grave. It's totally collapsed and flooded. God was with us today—"

"The family of Charlize Fullerton?" Morrow stopped talking and they all turned to where a doctor stood.

"That's me," Dillon said, standing, Lucy getting to her feet as well and nudged his leg. "That's us," he corrected.

The doctor didn't bat an eye at the sight of the men or the dog. "Agent Fullerton is a very lucky lady. Despite severe dehydration, cuts, and abrasions, four broken ribs, and a sprained wrist, she's going to be fine."

"Has she regained consciousness?" Dillon asked.

"Not yet, but she has a huge bump on the back of her head. The neurologist has looked at the CAT scan and isn't concerned about permanent damage."

"When can I see her?" Dillon asked.

The doctor shook his head. "They'll be moving her into ICU until she wakes up. You can see her then. But, I suggest you take the time to clean up." He stepped forward and held out his hand. "We've all heard what happened and I'd like to thank you and your team."

"We didn't save them all," Dillon said.

"Neither do we, but every one saved gives us the strength to go on." Dillon nodded and shook his hand. "There is a doctor's lounge down the hall. Feel free to make use of the shower."

Dillon thanked him and accepted a bag that Morrow held out. "A change of clothes and some toiletries. Get cleaned up. I'll be back but I need to speak to the families…"

Understanding that while he was waiting for his love to awaken, others were mourning the loss of theirs, Dillon nodded. "Thank you, Sir."

"No, thank you, Dillon."

Baxter shook Dillon's hand. "I can take Lucy. She can play with Casper. We're at the hotel just down the street."

Though the hospital staff had been gracious, Dillon knew it would be better all around if Lucy went with the team. He knelt and spent a few moments ruffling her fur. "You did good, Lucy. Go with Baxter—I'll stay with our girl."

Lucy licked his face and then trotted beside Baxter as they left the hospital. Dillon asked for directions to the lounge and was soon standing beneath the spray of the shower, his hands braced against the tile, his head bowed. A few more minutes would have seen Charlie among the dead but by God's grace, she was still with him. He said his thanks and made his promise that he'd spend every moment of the rest of his life loving her.

Despite the uncomfortable chair he'd pulled up next to her bed, the beeping of monitors, and the constant entry of nurses checking on their patient, Dillon was dozing. When he'd first entered the cubicle in ICU, his heart caught in his throat. Charlie looked so small and fragile, her skin as pale as alabaster except for the bruises that bloomed and the bandages covering the worst of the lacerations. He'd spoken to her quietly for hours but as the day turned into dawn, he'd finally bent forward to lay his head on the bed, quietly holding her hand. It was her fingers sliding through his hair that had him awakening, bolting to his feet.

"Charlie? Can you hear me, baby?"

Her eyelids fluttered and then opened, closing for a moment and opening again. "I knew you would find me," she rasped.

"I love you, Charlie. God, I love you so much. You're going to be fine."

"The others?"

Dillon stroked her hair off her face, knowing that to evade wouldn't make her rest. "We lost all but four. I'm not sure how many innocents died."

He watched tears fill her eyes before they closed and she gave a small nod. Bending, he kissed her gently. "I know, baby. Rest, Charlie, you rest now."

When she had slipped back into slumber, he went out and informed the nurses that she'd awakened. Within two hours, she'd awakened again and had been seen by the neurologist. By mid-afternoon, she was transferred to a private room, Dillon following her every step of the way. She remained hospitalized for another three days but refused to stay for the fourth.

"I need to be there," she demanded, her voice still a bit hoarse, but the headaches she'd suffered were diminishing a bit every day.

Dillon understood and helped her dress. He accepted a sheaf of papers with instructions for her continued care and then held her hand as an orderly wheeled her out of the hospital. Captain Morrow was waiting to take them to the first of many funerals. The church services were moving as agents were praised and family members spoke of their loved ones. It was absolutely heart-breaking standing at the graveside, watching coffins being lowered into the ground, each one holding a man or woman as well as their canine partner, all giving their lives in the service of others. He held Charlie as she cried, shedding his own tears at the loss of fellow agents.

When the last team had been laid to rest, they said their good-byes to Morrow. The team Dillon had flown down with had departed days earlier. He'd spoken with his director, informing him that he'd be staying and driving back with Charlie when she had recovered enough. The broken ribs were the worst of her injuries and though painful, would heal in time. They took a week to make the drive, stopping early to check into motels to allow her to sleep, Lucy curled up at her side of the bed, Dillon curled around her, holding her close.

CHAPTER 14

"*P*ut that bucket down!"

Charlie turned to see Dillon striding towards her. Ignoring his order, she tossed the tennis ball and watched as the puppies ran after it.

"Charlize Elena Fullerton, I said put it down. You should be in bed resting."

Rolling her eyes, she turned back to him. "Dillon, I swear I'm getting bedsores on my ass from all that fucking resting. It's been three months for Christ's sake! I'm fine!"

She heard Janet mutter, "Uh, oh," as Dillon opened the gate, his eyes narrowing as he strode across the exercise yard.

"You almost died—"

"But I didn't and I'm sick and tired of being treated like a piece of glass. I am not going to shatter!"

Her words didn't seem to be doing any good so she did the next best thing, she threw the next tennis ball at him. His eyes widened in shock as it smacked him in the chest. "Charlie, I'm warning you—"

Ignoring him, she tossed another and then another. Dillon batted them away, dodging balls and puppies who thought it was a great game as she began throwing them as fast as she could, backing up as he continued coming.

With the bucket empty, Charlie said, "I love you, Dillon, but if you don't back off, I swear I'll prove I'm fine by knocking you on your ass! I know my own body and the doctor cleared me weeks ago!"

Neither Dillon's glare nor his quirked eyebrow moved her. She stood, her hands on her hips, glaring right back. When she attempted to wag her own eyebrows, he'd cracked a smile and when she stomped her foot, he'd swooped her off her feet.

"Put me down!"

"Not going to happen. You're going straight to bed." When she began to twist, he added, "There's one way to prove you're fine and that's with me giving you a very thorough physical exam."

Charlie stilled and wrapped her arms around his neck. "Thank God. Though it's been so long I might need some instruction."

"I'm not waiting for you to buy some plaid skirt," Dillon said, his smile reaching his eyes. "But I am told that I'm a very good teacher."

A month later, they were wed beneath the trees where they'd had their picnic. Charlie wore a tea-length white dress that she and Martha had found in a vintage boutique in D.C. They said their vows, neither aware of anyone but each other and when the minister said, "You may kiss your bride," Dillon lifted his wife off her feet and kissed her until she was breathless. Their guests included Owen who had served as best man and Martha who was the maid-of-honor, Janet and her family, Baxter and his wife, Meredith. Several of Dillon's colleagues were in attendance as well as some of Dillon's friends from Black Light. Quilts were spread out on the grass and food was served from picnic baskets. Owen and Baxter helped pass out beverages of choice, all having been cooling in the pond. It was casual and it was perfect. That night, the newlyweds consummated their marriage and then lay in each other's arms.

"Thank you," Dillon said. When Charlie giggled, he bent to kiss her. "Not just for the incredible sex, Mrs. MacAllister, but for your gift."

Charlie looked across the room to where she'd hung the present. In a shadow box hanging on the wall, slightly soiled, white ropes lay against black velvet, the knot he'd fashioned... the one she'd held onto while waiting for him to find her, in the very center. She snuggled closer knowing that she didn't need the belt as their hearts and souls were connected.

Charlie had not attended the next training course Dillon gave at Quantico, but she was beside him as he drove through the gates of Quantico two weeks after their wedding. He parked the truck and before he opened the door, she laid a hand on his arm.

"Dillon, I want to prove myself. I don't want any special treatment. I want to be treated just like every one else in the class. Promise me you won't treat me any differently."

"On one condition," he said.

Charlie sighed but asked, "What condition?"

"Come on."

Charlie was busy running possibilities through her mind as they walked. When he led her into the building, she wasn't really paying attention but when she heard Lucy give a yip, she looked up to discover they were standing in the kennel.

"I know it's customary to bring the entire class in to pair them with their new partner, but, my condition is that you allow me to let you choose first." Charlie smiled and then reached up to plant a kiss on his lips. He kissed her back and then grinned. "None of that Agent MacAllister, people will think you're the teacher's pet."

Charlie watched as he opened each door of the dozen kennels. Dogs trotted out and then sat, waiting for further instructions. Charlie began to walk towards the dogs, as Dillon gave the signal to release. Some of the dogs ran to him, a couple ran towards Lucy, but one ran straight towards Charlie. By the time he reached her, she was on her knees, her arms open. The moment she wrapped her arms around his neck and his tongue came out to lick her cheek, they bonded.

Dillon walked over and squatted down beside them, ruffling the dog's fur. He had a huge grin on his face.

"Isn't he beautiful?" Charlie asked, taking the dogs face in her hands and smiling. "He has blue eyes!"

"Yes. Some people say that a dog with light colored eyes can see Heaven. He'll be your partner as well as your guardian angel."

"What's his name?"

Dillon smiled as Lucy came to sit beside them. "It couldn't be more perfect. Charlie, meet your new partner, Ricky."

Charlie looked at Dillon, then Lucy and then Ricky, and burst out into giggles, knowing it couldn't have been any other name.

* * *

"YOU'RE NOT READY YET?" Dillon asked, coming into their bedroom to see Charlie standing in nothing but her underwear. Not that he didn't enjoy the view, but he'd expected to leave a half-hour earlier.

"I can't decide what to wear," Charlie said, holding a sapphire blue dress in front of her and then replacing it with a red one.

Dillon walked to the closet and returned with the white dress she'd worn for their wedding. "Wear this."

"That's my wedding dress."

"Baby, I'm well aware of that, but you looked so stunning in it that I'd like to see you in it again."

Charlie smiled and was ready just a few minutes later. "Exactly where are we going?" she asked as he helped her into the truck.

"It's a surprise. A celebration of your graduation," Dillon said, dropping an arm around her as he drove towards D.C.

"I can't believe I'm now a certified K-9 agent. I can't thank Director Harrison enough for helping cut through the red tape involved in transferring my service."

"He's a good guy," Dillon agreed.

They ate at an Italian restaurant, Charlie tucking her napkin into the bodice of her dress. "Leave it to you to choose white when there's red spaghetti sauce involved," she said.

"To tell the truth, that never even entered my mind," Dillon confessed. As they ate, they talked about everything and nothing at all. After sharing a dish of tiramisu, Dillon pulled her chair out and took her hand. When he parked in a familiar parking lot, Charlie looked puzzled.

"Dillon, the club is closed on Mondays."

"Most Mondays, yes," Dillon said, taking her hand and leading her towards the shop. "But not tonight. Tonight is a gift from Jaxson, Chase, and Emma." He looked down and smiled. "Tonight, my love, is the night you learn to fly."

Once inside Black Light, he heard Charlie gasp as she saw the stage that had been prepared. While most of the club was in shadows, lights bathed the platform. Owen had coils of rope waiting and Martha, Emma, Jaxson, and Chase, were there to witness the artist in his creation.

Dillon removed his suit coat and slowly removed Charlie's dress, kissing down her body. He stripped her of everything, baring his canvas and leading her to the edge of the stage. "Kneel," he instructed softly.

Once she knelt before him, her eyes on him, he accepted a box from his brother. "I love you, Charlie. I will love you for the rest of our lives. We are man and wife, but tonight, I ask you to accept my collar." He opened the black, velvet box and watched as tears welled in her eyes as she saw what lay inside.

"Yes," Charlie said. "I accepted you as my husband, I am blessed to be your submissive as well."

Dillon took out the collar. It was an exact replica of the belt he'd placed around her waist, made of gold. The knot he'd tied to remind her they were connected even when apart, gleamed against her throat as he locked the collar around her neck. He pulled her up and kissed the golden knot as he'd done the rope one. Then he kissed his wife, his submissive before guiding her to the center of the stage. "Lay down and relax. Don't think, just give yourself over to me."

"I'm yours, Sir," she said softly.

Dillon began weaving the ropes around his wife's body, constantly checking her comfort as he bound her. A beautiful corset design ran across her arms that were bound behind her back. He crossed ropes around her breasts, the bonds enhancing their fullness, her nipples taut and waiting to be suckled. The pile of ropes diminished as he worked. He decorated each of her legs from thigh to ankle, and when he tied the last knot, he leaned over her.

"You are so very, very beautiful, and I am so very blessed to be your husband. I love you, Charlie."

"I love you, too, Dillon." She said, unable to touch him and yet her face, her eyes told of her love.

Dillon straightened and with a nod, Owen joined him. They began to pull on the ropes, lifting Charlie from the floor of the stage. She gasped as she swayed, but it wasn't a sound of distress. The smile on her lips as she allowed her head to fall back told of her pleasure.

Soft music began to play, the lights dimming a bit as Dillon began to caress her flesh that wasn't covered by rope. He bent to suckle on her nipples, her moans of pleasure magnified by the fact that her breasts were compressed, the blood flowing to them making her nipples so very sensitive. He kissed her belly and when she was whimpering, moaning in need, he moved to lift her head, to kiss her eyelids, her cheeks, her mouth.

As he slowly allowed her head to drop again, he stepped away. Dillon had never seen anything so beautiful as his wife. Wrapped in ropes that were so white against her flesh, the ink of her hair, the curl of her body, the rosiness of her nipples, the glistening of her sex. She was a masterpiece suspended in the air, trusting in her husband in every way. He gave a nod to Jaxson who smiled. Part of their gift was to provide a photographer to take photos— one that Dillon would choose to turn into a painting that would hang in their bedroom beside her wedding gift to him.

Once the photographer moved back, Dillon moved to begin again, kissing her deeply, watching her eyes open, the serenity in their depths making his heart skip a beat. He moved to stand between her legs and kissed her pussy. Long strokes of his tongue against the swollen folds of her sex had her making the sweetest mews. Dillon pushed her away, the swing of her body an erotic dance. He took his time, suckling, licking, nibbling until she was begging.

"Please, Sir, please... I need..."

"What, my love, what do you need?"

"You, Dillon, I need you."

Dillon needed her just as much. Unzipping his pants, he released his cock and pulled her towards him, sliding inside an inch at a time. They'd consummated their marriage weeks earlier, but tonight, they consummated their relationship as Dominant and submissive. Black Light was the perfect stage—for this incredible club was where their journey had truly begun.

The End

ABOUT THE AUTHOR

Maggie Ryan is a USA Today and #1 International Best Selling and Multi-award Winning Author in Victorian/ Historical, Contemporary and Western Erotic Romance

Fantasy is a world that offers endless possibilities. Whether you travel back in time to when the plains were open, take a journey to the cobblestone streets of London, take a stroll along the beach or walk through the streets of some foreign country, every letter of every word offers infinite possibilities. I love to write stories that take a reader on a journey, one they can disappear into and experience what might have been or what is to come. I never try to restrict myself to any one genre because there are just too many delicious possibilities out there and inside my head. I hope you will curl up in your favorite chair and take the journey with me. Happy Reading!

www.maggieryanauthor.com

ALSO BY MAGGIE RYAN

The Black Stallion Trilogy (With Alta Hensley)

Maddox, Book 1

Stryder, Book 2

Anson, Book 3

Women of Wintercrest series:

Louisa Revealed, Book 1

Lord Edward's Law, Book 2

Claimed, Book 3

Lucy Surrenders, Book 4

Hunter's Ridge series:

Lucy's Journey Home, Book 1

Homecoming, Book 2

Reunion, Book 3

Blessed Beginnings, Book 4

Hunter's Ridge Box Set

Divine Designs series:

Designed for Submission, Book 1

A Submissive's Dream, Book 2

Haven's Promise, Book 3

A Submissive's Gift, Book 4

Masters of the Castle series:

Rosie's Resolutions

Anthologies and Box Sets:

The Dark Forest

When the Gavel Falls (Masters of the Castle box set)

12 Naughty Days of Christmas Anthology 2014

Hero to Obey

Sweet Town Love

Single Titles:

Charming Isabella

Summer Solace

Becoming His: The Teaching of Rebecca

Treasured Submission

The Christmas Pickle

Realizing Her Dream (w/ Laurel Jane)

A Little Sunshine (written w/ Abbie Adams)

Leather and Grace

Please Daddy

Audio Books:

His Passionate Pioneer, Willamette Wives Book One

Louisa Revealed, Women of Wintercrest Book One

Lord Edward's Law, Women of Wintercrest Book Two

Claimed, Women of Wintercrest Book Three

Designed for Submission, Divine Designs Book One

A Submissive's Dream, Divine Designs Book Two

Lucy's Journey Home, Hunter's Ridge Book One

Homecoming, Hunter's Ridge Book Two

Treasured Submission

Charming Isabella

Summer Solace

Jewel's Gems

Lilly Blossoms

BLACK COLLAR PRESS

Did you enjoy your visit to Black Light? Have you read the other books in the series?

Infamous Love, A Black Light Prequel by Livia Grant
Black Light: Rocked by Livia Grant
Black Light: Exposed by Jennifer Bene
Black Light: Valentine Roulette by Various Authors
Black Light: Cuffed by Measha Stone
Coming Soon: Black Light: Rescued by Livia Grant

Black Collar Press is a small publishing house started by authors Livia Grant and Jennifer Bene in late 2016. The purpose was simple - to create a place where the erotic, kinky, and exciting worlds they love to explore could thrive and be joined by other like-minded authors.

If this is something that interests you, please go to the Black

Collar Press website and read through the FAQs. If your questions are not answered there, please contact us directly at: blackcollar-press@gmail.com.

WHERE TO FIND BLACK COLLAR PRESS:

- Website: http://www.blackcollarpress.com/
- Facebook: https://www.facebook.com/blackcollarpress/
- Twitter: https://twitter.com/BlackCollarPres

LET US KNOW WHAT YOU THINK

The art of writing can be a lonely activity at times. Authors sit alone, pouring their hearts into their stories, hoping readers will connect with their words and fall in love with their characters. It's easy to get discouraged at times.

And that's where you come in.

We'd sure appreciate it if you'd take a few minutes to leave a review to let us know what you thought of the story you just finished.

Thanks and happy reading!

Jennifer, Livia & Maggie